Nathanial Thatcher

The Wish Thieves

Nathanial Thatcher

The Wish Thieves

T. C. Chappell

Blue DOT Books

CONTENTS

Nathanial Thatcher

The Wish Thieves

Not so Long Ago and Across the Sea

"Come minette, to bed, it is time for another tale," said the elderly women with a French accent entangled in her rough Hebrew.

The brown curls of the pajama wearing six-year-old girl bounced excitedly to bed. She pulled the covers up to her chest and waited with anticipation.

"Are you ready to hear how the sprites collected a mountain of human eyelashes to string together the *Bridge of Ages!*"

The young girl giggled and nodded enthusiastically.

"Good," the old women said with a smile and pulled her shawl in close. "Now, before this bridge, the sprites of Horusberg had only gathered the eyelashes that fell naturally from the humans they followed about, which was a pretty dull way to spend an afternoon as you can imagine, but this project was one for the history books and it was going to take some picking to get it done on time."

"It started as one or two extra eyelashes pulled from those who weren't shedding adequately and that seemed harmless enough, but by the end of the week the whole human town had an eyelash-dropping epidemic, or so they thought the poor things. They even gave it a name, Madarosis they called it! The truth of it was, of course, the sprites own impatience, and what they did not realize was that by stripping an eyelid clean of all its lashes, it would take twice as long for them to grow back. The project hit hard delays from their miscalculation and something had to be done about it!"

"Did they learn their lesson, Mataunte? Did they have to wait for the town people's lashes to grow back and have them fall out naturally again?"

"No minette. They went to the adjacent town and took all of those townspeople's eyelashes to finish their bridge. These stories are to remind you of the impatience and greed of those who play their tricks on you. Always remember. The sprites never learn, they just move on."

"Oh," the little girl said with a sigh, and after a moment of contemplation she whispered, "Papa says your stories are bobbemyseh and not to listen, Mataunte."

"Your papa has tricked eyes too and he's not to blame for his ignorance. He did not have a mataunte to tell him the way. It is important however that you learn the truth of things, for you more than he must know it. Knowledge is the key to all things." The old woman stood and bent over to kiss the girl's forehead. "Goodnight, my little minette."

"Goodnight, Mataunte."

Mataunte went toward the door and flipped off the light switch.

"Mataunte," the girl called out into the darkness.

"Yes?"

"Why do you think I need to know these things more than Papa?"

"Because minette, one day the trick on your eyes will fail, and when that day comes, you will need to know."

Birthday Cake or
a Big Mistake

Suzy Thatcher prepared for her son's twelfth birthday in the manner a scientist prepares a clean room. A white mask covered her nose and mouth, obscuring her pale oval face. She doused the house with an aerosol to kill *99% of germs* and disinfecting wipes to squash the rest. Her brown ponytail swished in time with her foggy strokes throughout the kitchen, living room, one and a half bathrooms, her bedroom and even the linen closet, before she took one more sweep over every already shiny surface concluding at Nathanial's bedroom door.

Inside the room, Nathanial paced anxiously. He pulled his fingers across the books, which covered two entire walls.

Handmade labels of History, Science, and Mathematics clicked along with him in the School Stuff section. Fantasy, Action, and Sci-fi took their turns in the Cool Stuff section. Finally, he reached the end in Places I Will Go, and Sports to Try.

A Kinect Sports game was paused on a wall-mounted TV until Nathanial pushed the glowing Xbox button with his big toe, sending the screen to black. He froze there, about to cough, but then forcefully gulped down his held breath.

"Not today," he ordered himself.

Nathanial collapsed over his balled up comforter and stared upside down at the blanketed wall above him. Staring back was a map of the world, the snow kissed Rocky Mountains and mysterious mists swimming at the base of a giant pagoda. Favorite movie posters, such as *Pirates of the Caribbean* and *The Goonies* were collaged around two doors, one leading to a small bathroom and the other out toward his ever-elusive freedom.

Groaning like a caged tiger, Nathanial looked to Jupiter on his ceiling and pretended he was on the planet with its immense gravity pulling him heavily out of bed.

"Mo-om, come on, can I come out yet?" Nathanial called impatiently.

Suzy bounced nervously at the door while dousing her arms with sanitizer. She put her hand on the goth painted sign that said, *Cube of Solitude*, then moved her finger to the Release button on the door side panel. The glowing readings of Humidity, Air Quality, and Temperature went dark and steam exuded from the hinges. With successive pops the door gave way and Suzy pulled.

"Happy birthday darling," she said forcing excitement beyond her anxiety.

Nathanial hesitated, unbelieving, until he let the sight wash over him like the uncontainable smile crossing his cheeks. He ran and tackled Suzy with a hug, then looked up to her face mask.

"You don't have to wear that, do you?"

"It's better if I do," she said rubbing his shaggy blonde head.

"You're not sick and I haven't coughed yet today. Let's give it a shot."

Suzy held her breath. "Okay," she said and skeptically pulled off the mask. The magnitude of that simple gesture sparkled between their eyes. "Come on," Suzy said and pulled Nathanial ecstatically from the room.

Two large polka-dotted candles, in the shape of a one and a two, burned atop a double-decker cheesecake on the kitchen table. Nathanial positioned himself in front of the cake and rubbed his hands together with anticipation.

"Hold your breath, make a wish, blow out ALL the candles in one huff, and your wish could come true!" Suzy said, excited.

Nathanial laughed. "Ma, there's only two candles. I think I can handle it."

"I know, I know. I did that on purpose this year, just to be sure you could."

"You're so funny," Nathanial said shaking his head. He closed his eyes and took a deep breath. His cheeks puffed out with concentration.

Suzy watched him with a smile. He concentrated so intently on his wish and she knew the words he was reciting in his mind. It was a wish for everything she had tried to, but been unable to make come true. Her smile faded at the feeling of failure.

Nathanial quickly opened his eyes and blew on the flames with all of his might until the fire was snuffed out and the candles were smoking. With a toothy grin, he looked up to his mom who quickly put her smile back into place and wiped away a beginning tear. She clapped enthusiastically.

"Yay! Happy birthday old man!" she laughed. "Let's cut the cake!" She picked up a knife and handed it to Nathanial. "You should have the honors."

Nathanial gawked. "Really!" He took the knife. She had never let him cut the cake before. He felt the weight of the knife in his hand and licked his lips as he readied the blade upon the cake, but suddenly, his face contorted and he buried it into his elbow with a, "cough, cough, cough".

Like lightning, Suzy grabbed the knife out of Nathanial's hand. He dropped his arm heavily and stared at the ground.

"We should get you back into your room," Suzy stated.

"No Mom," he protested.

"I'll bring you a slice in there."

"Mom, please."

"I really shouldn't have taken off the mask."

"Don't say that."

She took the cake to the counter. "You better go before it gets worse." She pulled a clean mask from a box by the cutting board and put it on.

"Mom, please listen to me. I'm doing much better. I only coughed thirteen times yesterday. Can you believe it?" but his attempt to reinstate hope only met a shaking head.

Suzy pulled the sanitizer from her jeans pocket and rubbed it over her arms again. "You know that's because…"

"Because my room is sterile, I know."

"And the second you leave your room…"

"I know, Mom, but please, I need to get out of there."

"You'll pick up whatever micro-baddy might be floating around from a cold ten years old."

"Seriously Mom, let's just go on a day trip, to the park, to a store, to the mailbox!"

"Nathanial," Suzy said turning to him seriously, "do you want to become the bubble boy?"

"I am the bubble boy!" he screamed and a severe cough abruptly ended the argument. Nathanial could not catch his breath.

Suzy dropped the sanitizer, rushed over and helped her son to his feet. With each step, the intensity of the cough grew stronger until it was difficult for Suzy to keep ahold of him.

Careening through his bedroom door, Nathanial crumpled to the floor as Suzy exited, slammed the door, and hit Purge on the exterior panel. Steam exuded from the door cracks.

The bedroom's bordering vents made a loud sucking noise and then kicked out a tumbling haze that fell as a smoke waterfall to the floor.

Nathanial ran to the bathroom in a coughing fit and hovered over the sink.

Suzy put her hand on the wall at the end of the hallway. She listened to her son coughing and closed her eyes tight, seeing herself beside him in her mind's eye.

"It'll pass baby, just breathe," she yelled at the wall.

Nathanial took hold of his breath and

mentally ordered it all to stop. His face went red, then blue and purple. His lungs were ready to burst and his head was swimming. He heard his mom pounding on the wall, ordering him to *"breathe"* but with each breath would come a cough and he just wanted it to stop!

The trapped air burst free and Nathanial took a breath. In a moment of peace, he caught his reflection and shook his head.

"It comes on so fast," he whispered.

Dark circles glared under his brown eyes and sweat dampened the curls around his pale forehead.

The panel by Nathanial's door started flashing. A warning read, *Humidity Low.* Suzy growled at the display and yelled, "Nathanial, I need to run out for some liquid treatment for the humidifier. Just lie down, honey."

"Okay...Mom," he yelled back between coughs.

A fever made the voyage from head to foot and Nathanial plunged into the faucet's cool waterfall. He pulled the hand towel off its hook, determined to smother the oncoming cough.

Stumbling to the full body mirror, Nathanial drooped and leaned into his reflection, pressing his forehead onto the smooth glass.

He stared down at his doppelganger toes, wiggled them, and blinked to pull them into focus, but his limbs were Jell-O and the world was wobbly. Nathanial knew he only had one sweet clear breath remaining before the cascade of coughs would win. He braced for impact, crumbled down onto the floor and blacked out.

"Why won't this thing start?" said a small Brooklyn accented voice.

"You must be doing it wrong," said another male voice.

Nathanial opened his eyes, still on the bathroom floor. He stared up at the ceiling and groaned.

"There we go, there we go," exclaimed the first voice. "Now we're talkin'!"

Nathanial slowly stood and stumbled to his room to turn off his TV, but it wasn't on.

"All right, let's see, do a li'l bit here and a tug there…" the Brooklyn voice continued.

A strange sensation clogged Nathanial's throat. He quickly ran to the sink and hocked up a loogie.

"Bea-u-ti-ful!" the voice yelled.

Nathanial shook his head and cleaned out his ears.

"Uhh, Phlegm," the second voice spoke up again.

"That stuff makes for the best *Grit the Gook*," the Brooklyn voice dubbed Phlegm said enthusiastically.

"Phlegm, wait," warned the second voice but it was too late.

Phlegm jumped down off some place near Nathanial's shirt collar, causing him to flinch, and landed in the sink where he started collecting Nathanial's loogie. Nathanial curled his nose on closer inspection of the grimy named humanoid, Phlegm. The name seemed purposefully suited to him. His skin was the same color as the substance he now put in a vile, corked, and hung onto his jumpsuit work-belt. About an inch tall, Phlegm had jagged-edged ears, dark green slicked-back hair and brown oval eyes.

"What the…?" Nathanial said with a jump back, but Phlegm still didn't seem to notice that *he* had been noticed. When a second slightly taller humanoid flew from somewhere behind Nathanial's ear, Nathanial couldn't help but have a quick spaz-out moment. He brushed at his ears and hair, punched at his shirt and swiped down his pants before he heard the new little man trying to get his attention.

"Hey, hey, hey, calm down," he said.

Nathanial stopped and stared at the blue thing hovering in front of him. He had wings, unlike Phlegm. His skin was light blue. His thick brushed-back hair was dark blue, almost black. His eyes were a sparkling chlorine pool blue and his suit and tie were navy blue.

Nathanial looked back down at Phlegm, who was staring dumbfounded back up at him.

"Boss," Phlegm squeaked up, "why is the Factory looking at me?"

The blue guy being called Boss waved the question away signaling Phlegm to stay quiet. "Hello," he said attempting a smile at Nathanial.

Nathanial looked back up to him.

"I see that, uh, you can see us now," he started again uncertainly.

Nathanial nodded.

"Don't be alarmed," he said gliding down to the sink edge where Phlegm had climbed up. When he touched down it was much like a grasshopper landing. His top wing flaps were solid blue and they merged perfectly to his suit to appear more like coattails than wings.

"This is my co-worker, Phlegm," he said gesturing beside him.

"That's right," Phlegm piped up. "Hellooo, Mr. Factory!"

Boss elbowed him.

"Ow," he mumbled rubbing his side and then cleared his throat. "I mean Mr...Natha, Nathany, Nathani-AL!"

"Why does he keep calling me *Factory*?" Nathanial asked.

"Oh, don't worry about that," said Boss laughing and waving a hand in the air. "Let's just get this sorted out, shall we? Now,

I realize it's your twelfth birthday today; is that right?"

"Yeah, so?" Nathanial shrugged.

"Yeah, what you gettin' at, Boss?" Phlegm queried.

Boss rolled his eyes at Phlegm and continued, "What kind of cake was it that you had there?" Boss asked brightening his smile.

"Cheesecake. Why?" Nathanial responded shortly.

"OHHH," exclaimed Phlegm wide-eyed. "Cheesecake, that dirty playing, no good sprite, when I get my hands on her… ouch!" He got another elbow in the side.

"And what exactly did you wish when you blew out your candles?" Boss pressed on holding his smile as nicely as he could.

Nathanial narrowed his eyes. "Why? Who are you guys? WHAT are you guys? Why does it matter what my cake was or what I wished for?"

Boss dropped his smile and patient demeanor. "Look kid, do you want us to disappear or not?"

"I don't know. I don't know anything

about you. What were you doing on my shirt and why was he collecting my, my... yuck?" Nathanial shook from the thought.

Phlegm tugged his jumpsuit collar and said, "Hey, you don't know yuck till you've been down in the dregs, Mr. Factory Man. Now tell us your wish and move on."

"No," Nathanial said flatly.

"Why?" asked Phlegm and Boss in unison.

"Because."

"Because why?"

"Everyone knows if you tell your wish it won't come true," Nathanial said rolling his eyes.

Both Phlegm and Boss slapped hands to their faces and shook their heads.

"Oh boy," Boss said brushing his fingers through his thick hair. "Then there's only one thing we can do."

Now Phlegm and Nathanial asked in unison, "What?"

"We have to take him through the Niche to headquarters."

"Headquarters?!" Phlegm gasped. "That's a little drastic, don't you think?"

"What headquarters?" Nathanial asked,

but Boss only addressed Phlegm.

"He's our biggest producer on the east coast. You know we can't lose him."

"What are you talking about, lose him? He's right here, ain't he?" reasoned Phlegm.

"Look at your watch." Boss sighed.

"Yeah, so?" Phlegm glanced down to his wrist. "It's about quittin' time."

"Now look at your belt."

He did as told, then screamed, "Geez Louise, I ain't met my quota!"

"Exactly. Now do you think we can go about business as usual with him chatting and swatting at us?" Boss asked with raised eyebrows.

"Whelp, that's why I call you, Boss. You're totally right, as usual." Phlegm nodded then turned to Nathanial to say, "Looks like you're coming with us Factor.., oh-a, kid!"

"What? I can't go with you. I can't go *anywhere*. If I leave my room, I get horrible coughing attacks. It could kill me! I've never even opened the window. Look for yourself, it's painted shut. And if I could leave my room I wouldn't be going off to some headquarters with two strange little things like you that are obviously up to something fishy with my wish."

Boss flew up to Nathanial's eye level and said, "Hey, I understand this freaks you out, but I assure you, if you come with us, speak to our boss—"

"I thought you were the boss," Nathanial interrupted.

"No, I just call him that," Phlegm piped in. "He's got one of those nameless curses on him, you know, where he can't tell you his real name, so I just…"

"Phlegm, please, that's enough," Boss said hastily, and then turned to Nathanial, "You just need to speak to our boss. You'll be fine as long as you're with me. No cough attacks, I assure you. Your mom won't even know you're gone. You'll get a wish, and when we get you back home everything will be normal again."

Nathanial chewed on his tongue for a moment. "I don't know. That all sounds a little impossible if you ask me. How can you promise me I won't have a cough attack?"

Phlegm shook his head and whispered behind his hand to Boss, "this one's a little slow in the attic if you know what I mean."

Boss thinly smiled at Nathanial and said, "Well, Nathanial, because your wish was granted."

Nathanial gawked and his heart skipped a beat. "How?" He finally asked, daring himself to believe. "I mean, are you like leprechauns or fairy god…fathers or what? You said sprite earlier, is that it? You do look kinda' like something I read about once, but it's weird, you're wearing a suit. Shouldn't you be dressed in leaves or something?"

Phlegm snorted.

Boss let his small smile grow until his broad grin answered. "If you're impressed by our mastering of textiles, just you wait. We share many inventions with your kind and beyond. We have unique abilities giving us advantages that you wouldn't believe. Come with us if you want to see for yourself."

Nathanial lifted his eyebrows. Boss had found his curiosity button and pushed it dead on, though it wasn't yet enough to kill his caution.

"But you want me to talk to your Boss about my wish? You think he doesn't want me to have it, don't you? You want him to take it away from me." He said suspiciously.

"A wish is due to you, no need talk about that, but I know he won't be happy that you can see us," Boss said seriously, "and it's for your own good that you don't. You can't be the only human around without the trick on your eyes. They'll lock you in the loony bin if they catch you talking to us. I've seen it happen before."

The butterflies in Nathanial's stomach were on the verge of escape. He was afraid to trust these two little men. It all seemed too good to be true as they held this silver platter of dreams before him. If he truly did have his health, what more did he ever want with that gift than to go on adventures, and here was an adventure. In all of his years of planning, he had never come close to concocting one as exotic as this.

"I guess I shouldn't start my new life turning down opportunities. I mean, if you think he's just going to make it so I can't see you, that should be fine." Nathanial finally said with a grin.

"That's the spirit." Boss winked.

IN EVERY CORNER THERE'S A NICHE

Nathanial knelt on one knee at the place where his bookshelves met his DVD shelf and finished tying his bright white sneakers. He smiled admiringly at them before curiously watching Boss fly between the *Harry Potter* books and *Harry Potter* movies and knock in the corner where they met.

"Hey, Bunny. Could use a little dust out here," Boss yelled.

Nathanial looked to Phlegm who sat on his shoulder. Phlegm kicked towards the corner as if to say, *look there not at me, you big oaf.* He was obviously grumpy about the way the day was turning out.

A four-inch by four-inch square door swung open cutting the books and movies through their middles. A fuzzy-headed, bronze-faced, scruffily dressed, cat-eyed, inch tall girl stood in the opening.

"What'd you say there, Bossy Man? You need some dust?" she asked and smirked at Boss before taking notice of Nathanial staring down at her. This made her thoroughly uncomfortable. "Ugh, Boss, he's looking right at me."

"I know. That's why we need the dust," Boss said nodding.

"Oh," perked up Bunny. "No problem!"

She held out her hands, bent her head over them, shook like a wet pup and caught the sparkles that fell from her fluffy hair before blowing the small pile toward Nathanial.

Phlegm quickly jumped from Nathanial's shoulder into the Niche.

Nathanial took in one mighty breath, and with a single tingling sneeze popped up into the air, shrinking until he was not even an inch tall, only to be caught by Boss and thrown into the corner's Niche.

The landing was rough and unceremonious. From the floor, Nathanial watched the corner door that protruded towards him closing. It read *Lyso* on the left and *Torium* on the right. He could just barely see his giant room vanish from sight and fear sickened him. This was it. His room was on the other side of that door; the place that had kept him alive his entire life. Timidly he inhaled and exhaled. Where there would have been a cough that morning, now there erupted a giant smile.

"Boss, I'll catch you later. I'm going to turn in what we got even if it ain't all that impressive," said Phlegm from behind Nathanial.

"Sure," Boss waved him off. "Let's go," he said and helped Nathanial to his feet.

Nathanial stabilized, looked at his hands, body and feet, then UP at Boss. "Whoa, you're big," he said stupefied by this new stature.

Bunny poked him in the tummy and said, "You're small, Natey my man!"

"You know my name?" Nathanial asked with surprise.

"Course I do. I've been working your Niche for years! I'm Bunny!" She stuck out her hand. Nathanial took it to receive one firm how-do-you-do shake, before the conundrum around him stole back his attention.

He walked between Boss and Bunny, through a city that was several stories high and made from bits of everything. Light posts glowed without the need of flame. Paper Mache had been molded into shops, quarters had replaced the wheel spokes of a passing bicycle, socks had been made into waste bins, buttons were sold as hats, and beautiful homes were carved right into the wood of what Nathanial assumed was the inside walls of his house!

Nathanial spotted one sprite leaving his home by means of a strange elevator basket. His eyes followed the rope tied to this basket down a pulley system that connected to a massive hamster wheel driven by a mouse with bunny-like hindquarters. Some homes sat just above the shops and had stairway entries, but the higher he gazed with his neck craned, the more homes he found were only reachable by flying. Doors faced out to thin air with no stairs or lift to reach them.

This made Nathanial wonder about… what had Phlegm called them, sprites? Why did some have wings and others didn't?

Why were there so many different colors and different types?

He watched the hustle and bustle around him. Some sprites wore suits like Boss but most compiled their clothing of random bits of plastic, paper, leaves, sticks, furs, flowers, cotton balls and twine. Nathanial thought about Boss's textile remark and figured if he had a choice between a manufactured suit and a hodgepodge outfit made from bits of everything, he'd take the latter too!

Nathanial's attention was then drawn to a squatting purple sprite digging in a bin, which looked suspiciously like one of his superhero socks. Bunny followed Nathanial's gaze and yelled, "Hey June!"

June looked startled and made to run.

"I see you," Bunny called.

June pushed the bin over and headed off. Bunny jumped after her and tackled her a few sprinting steps away from the knocked over bin.

Boss pulled Nathanial away as he tried to stop and see what Bunny was wrestling out of June's hands.

"Don't mind that. Just business," Boss said

and he pulled Nathanial more forcefully ahead.

After walking a few blocks, Nathanial noticed a reoccurring sale item in many of the shop windows. Lined up by the dozens were bright yellow spray bottles. The words Grit the Gook boldly labeled this obviously popular product. It's slogan, *With this true grit, what gook can stans-it?* was advertised on windows, posters, and many stand-up boards along the path.

A young, pale, almost translucent skinned sprite in a flat cap and overalls, held up the product at his own bottle stacked stand yelling, "Get your grit gone with the best deal anywheres, right here, fresh from the source, Grit the Gook, whole-sale, no better deal, multi-purpose use! You gotta mess? Grit the Gook. You gotta top that won't pop? Grit the Gook. You want a look to get the looks. Grit the Gook. Spray it in your hair for a shine, and you'll be looking just fine!"

"Wait a second," Nathanial thought out loud. "Grit the Gook. Isn't that what Phlegm said?"

Boss stopped. Nathanial, caught by

surprise, bumped into Boss and dropped his thought.

"This is it," Boss said.

Nathanial looked to the building in front of him and almost did a back bend trying to see the top that vanished into darkness. He imagined looking up at the Empire State Building, a place that was on his top ten must visit list, might feel very similar.

"What is this place?" he asked in awe.

"Headquarters, of course," Boss replied.

"Oh, that was fast. What's it headquarters of exactly?"

"Oh," Boss sighed, "everything."

They stepped into a large vaulted room through tall slender doors. Before them stretched a reception desk from wall to wall. Behind it sat merely one, single, pink, pointy-eared sprite whose ears weren't just pointy; they were a good length above her cotton candy hair pointy. Nathanial couldn't stop staring at them as they approached her in the otherwise empty room.

"He's expecting you," her voice echoed in the cavern-like space.

A portion of the desk slid into itself beside

the receptionist leaving an opening. A sound of gushing wind filled the room. Nathanial peered into the opening and saw a hole beneath him. His hair flew upward in the wind spouting from the darkness below.

"I don't understand." Nathanial gulped. "Are we supposed to go down there?"

The receptionist giggled.

"It's okay," Boss said. "Take my hand."

Nathanial did so uncertainly.

"When I say so, just take a step," Boss said with a nod.

They were right on the edge of the dark chasm. Taking a step did not seem like a good idea, but Nathanial remembered what Boss had said. As long as he's with Boss, he should be fine, or at least he knew Boss would be fine, and he gripped tighter to the sprite's hand.

"Okay." Boss nodded again. "Now."

They took a step. Amazingly they did not fall but instead, with a lurch of the stomach, they shot up into the air. For a moment Nathanial was blinded by light. He was pretty sure they were outside but it was only a few seconds of complete confusion and fear before they landed on a balcony.

Nathanial's legs were like rubber and he sat down accordingly. Boss lifted him back up just as Nathanial's vision started to adjust to the light and he saw they were at the tip of a massive dirigible. Before he could even mutter the word "wow" he was being pulled through large brass doors.

The light in the room was just as intense as outside. Nathanial rubbed his eyes and took a second stab at focusing. A desk sat silhouetted by the one window that stretched the length of the room. Behind the desk stood the largest sprite in both height and girth that Nathanial had yet to see. This giant of a sprite took his three-fingered hand from its place on the window and clasped it in his other hand behind his back.

"So this is the lucrative Nathanial Thatcher," the deep voice stated to the silent room. "The largest Lysozyme factory on the east coast."

Nathanial furrowed his brows and opened his mouth. With a quick squeeze on his shoulder, Boss warned him to stay quiet.

"I understand today is your twelfth birthday," the sprite stated.

Nathanial looked to Boss, who nodded.

"Yes, Sir," he responded.

"And you made a wish as you blew out your candles."

"That's right."

"Tell me. When was your first memory of making such a wish?"

Nathanial hesitated.

"Let me simplify the question. Can you remember ever making any other wish? The wish you made today, it's your only wish."

Nathanial swallowed hard.

"I don't need you to answer. I know," said the giant male figure as he turned toward him. "Come here."

Nathanial timidly approached and was baffled to stand only as high as the sprite's belt.

"What do you see out the window?" he asked with a gesture out beyond the glass.

Nathanial looked out and his jaw parted. "Whoa," he muttered.

It was his town. He never thought he'd see it from such a height. Directly below was his house. Surrounding it were about twenty other homes, the courthouse perched up on the hill and Main Street stretched out from it for two whole stoplights.

"It's my town," he said looking straight down to get a better peek at his house. Was his mother home yet?

"Look closer." The sprite handed Nathanial a strange pair of binocular-like spectacles with knobs on the temple.

Nathanial put them on. "This is crazy. I can see right up to the houses."

"What else do you see? Look down at your house."

Nathanial did so and the man turned a knob on the spectacles. The image zoomed in even more.

"Geez," Nathanial exclaimed amazed. "Wait, what are those?"

Sprites were all over the place. A couple seemed to be scraping green stuff off the roof of his house. He panned his head over to the sidewalk and saw at least one sprite on every person, two on a dog, and yet another windsurfing above a car that drove by.

"Sprites, right?" Nathanial answered himself. "Man, they are everywhere."

"That's because this is our town too," the

man said taking the specs off Nathanial.

Nathanial got a good look at his face for the first time and didn't like what he saw. This did not look like a sprite or a man. He had rough skin, multi-colored brown, green and yellow, no hair and a bulbous nose. The expensive suit did not seem to go with the feeling of him.

"I don't understand," Nathanial managed to say. "What does this have to do with me?"

At this moment, a tall dark figure side-stepped into the room from a corner door and hung there. Everyone looked over to him, but with the big man's dismissal of the new presence, the focus went back on Nathanial.

"Every human gives purpose to our kind. You have been especially useful. Tell me what you wished for," said the large sprite seriously.

"But you seem to know," Nathanial murmured backing away.

"Tell me," he said advancing on Nathanial.

Trying to be brave Nathanial stopped backing away and asked, "Why?"

This was the first time in Nathanial's life

that he was out doing something. The first time he was seeing and experiencing new things, and it was the first time he *believed* that telling someone what he wished for might actually forfeit his wish! He wasn't about to give that up to some bully, at least not without a detailed explanation and good reason.

The giant man set down the binocular specs and started to move his warty three fingers toward Nathanial.

Boss stepped in quickly. "Sir, no need to pressure the boy. Just came for permission to take him to Midtown. We already tried to get him to tell us the wish. He won't do it. His mother really ingrained in him those superstitions, the ones that were once law to all kind. He isn't letting up on the wish one," his ramble hastened, "and it's still *our* law, after all. In fact, he won't even go under a ladder or open an umbrella in the house, really, you'd think..."

"Yes, yes," the boss of Boss waved him quiet with impatience. He looked as though the next words were really hard to say. "Take him then."

"Thank you, Sir," said Boss with a quick tug on Nathanial's arm and led him all the way out the brass doors they had entered through.

The large man turned back to the window and put his hand up onto the glass.

"You know what to do," he said with a grumble, and the tall man in the corner exited after Boss.

THE ARGOSY

After a stomach plunging return to the ground within a leaf-structured capsule, Boss hurried Nathanial out of the headquarters building.

"Alright, transport, let's see," Boss muttered to himself with increased agitation.

"Hey," Nathanial said, trying to get a hold of the situation. "What just happened back there?" but Boss wasn't listening.

Boss spotted a booth with an old man sitting behind it and went straight for it.

"Boss," Nathanial tried again hurrying to keep up, "you hear me? What did you mean you came for permission to take me some other place? You said headquarters, not this other place! You said we'd be home before my mom got back. This wasn't the deal!"

Boss reached the old man who would

look like a beggar if he hadn't been selling something. His long gray unkempt beard had bits of twig in it and his furry twisted hat kept twitching.

"Two for the Argosy please," Boss said to the toothless geezer as he reached into his pocket for some coin.

"Make that three," Phlegm said running in and throwing down two gold pieces and a silver. "Tried to salvage what I could back at processing but the future's lookin' grim unless we get him fixed."

"Make that four," smiled Bunny tossing something small and squeaky at the old man's hat, which shockingly caught Bunny's toss and engulfed it into its furry recesses.

Everyone looked to her quizzically.

"What?" She shrugged. "I have a sister in Midtown. That's where you're headed, right?"

Boss nodded and went back to his exchange with the old man.

"No wait," Nathanial said as the old man pushed over four tickets, "make it three. I'm not going." He pushed one of the tickets back defiantly.

The old man started to take it back but Boss

grabbed it and said, "Just a sec." He turned to Nathanial. "Look, you have no idea what we just barely got away from in there."

"If you explain it to me then maybe—" Nathanial started but Boss held up his hand.

"I know you think we made a deal back in your room. You talk to my boss, we get you home before your mom notices, you get a wish, and everyone's happy, right?"

"Right." Nathanial nodded sternly.

"Well, Nathanial, I have to tell you, I didn't take you for a spunk," Boss said a little impressed, a little annoyed.

"What?" Nathanial asked impatiently.

"I thought the big man would ask you once what that wish of yours was, you'd spill the beans and that'd be that. We'd all go back to normal."

"Normal? Do you know what normal is for me? It's not normal! You said he'd just make it so I couldn't see you. You said I'd keep my wish!" Nathanial protested with his hands on his hips.

"I said you'd get a wish, not necessarily your current wish." Boss said with a sigh and pinched the bridge of his nose. "And that part of the deal would only need to come into play if you didn't 'spill the beans' so to speak, which is where we find ourselves now."

"So what are you saying? You lied?"

"I gambled," Boss said pointedly, "and lost. Wouldn't be the first time. But now that you've made it clear how stubborn you are, we must go through with the deal to it's fullest and most tiresome extent, but you have to come with me if you want a wish."

"I don't want a wish I want *MY* wish. The wish that's already been granted! It's the only thing I've ever wanted and so far, it's more than I could have ever dreamed it to be. It's amazing, and you want to take it away from me? Why? Why is this so important to you?"

"It's our livelihood and you're messing with it kid. Just listen to me for a second." Boss bent down and put a hand on Nathanial's shoulder. "That sprite in there has ways of getting you to confess your wish and make it obsolete," he said gesturing to the building they just ran from. "Believe it or not I don't want this to go down that way. You deserve a wish, but that sprite up there doesn't care if you have one. He's looking for the quickest way to get production back on schedule. Let me take you to Midtown. We can make an exchange. You'll have some time to come up with another wish, and we'll be there to make sure it works for everyone this time, not just you, but for all of us. I know that might sound harsh, asking you not to be selfish with this decision, but everything you see around here relies on you. It's a lot to ask but together we can come up with a solution, a compromise. "

"Listen to him, Factory Nathan. Midtown is the better deal," Phlegm said nodding.

Nathanial groaned. He wasn't sure what choice he really had in the matter. If he refused then he'd most likely be handed back over to the green blob in the sky for a wish removal, yet trying to imagine an exchange seemed quite as bad. If there had been any other wish worth making, he would have made it on at least one other occasion, but he never had; not on one star, not on one eyelash, not on any birthday had he ever wished for anything different. But was he being selfish? Did this entire town really rely on him giving up his dream?

He thought about his mother and how much she had done for him. She wasn't selfish. She'd dedicated her life to trying to make him better. The eternal optimist who always let him out on his birthday to see if his immune system had strengthened over the year. Always believing that this year would be the year the doctors had promised her when he was a baby. That finally his body would adapt. If only she could see him now. He wanted to ask her advice in that moment. Would she sacrifice a town for him?

"What about my mom?" he asked with her still in his thoughts. "You said I'd be back in time…"

"I said she wouldn't notice you were gone," Boss corrected. "There's a memory draft over your house. It's an auto-response to a human going through a Niche. While you're away, she'll be in a kind of daze, like a lazy forgetfulness. Most humans these days binge watch on Netflix to cope with the effects. On your return your absence will feel like nothing more than a dream to her."

"Man," Nathanial said shaking his head,

"you sprites really are tricky creatures, aren't you?"

Phlegm snorted. "Just the tip of the wings, kid."

"So what'll it be then?" The old man croaked so loudly and suddenly his hat almost jumped off his head. "Is it three or four?"

Boss stood up and looked at Nathanial for his answer.

Nathanial nodded, "Four." He thought it better to continue on this adventure rather than turn away in fear of none to come.

Boss smiled and patted Nathanial on the back.

The old ticket seller jumped off his stool revealing himself to be a foot shorter than Nathanial. He gestured to the quartet to follow him. They went through his luggage shop stacked with suitcases crafted of shell, from both tree and sea. Cramped between the back shelves hid a spiraled staircase that they single filed their way down before exiting into a cave-like basement.

"Tickets please," the little old man shouted.

Boss gave him back the tickets. The geezer stacked them and rammed them halfway into his hat. There was a *crunch*. When he pulled the tickets back out they looked as if the shark from *Jaws* had used them for a snack. He handed Boss the chomped tickets.

"Now give those to the captain of the Argosy when you get there and be quick about it! They're loading while you dilly dolly about here in front of me!"

He unlocked a giant padlock that dangled off a wooden arched door set deeply into the stone. An ancient screech protested with its opening. Nathanial peered down the revealed tunnel, which mimicked its doorframe in shape. He gawked at the stretching darkness with but a pinprick of light at its end.

"What do you think, should Nate-a-rino go first?" Bunny said giggling.

"What, why?" Nathanial asked suspiciously.

"Absolutely," Phlegm rang out.

"Tuck-and-roll," the old man said before head butting Nathanial in the back, forcing him through the door.

There was a gigantic lurch that pulled every

organ, including and most disturbingly his skin, in all outward directions as he zoomed through the windy darkness. All Nathanial could do to keep from screaming was to concentrate on the growing light and believe with all of his might that when he reached it the sensation would stop.

It was as sudden a stop as it had been a start. Nathanial stood on a bright grassy hilltop in the middle of nowhere. Judging by the surroundings he appeared to be normal sized again. He took a few uneven steps forward and it was a good thing he did too, as Bunny appeared exactly where he had just been. She grabbed him by the shoulders and jumped, giggling, away. Then Phlegm popped into place, quickly stepped aside, and finally Boss appeared.

To Nathanial's awe, everyone had changed.

"You guys look almost normal," he said eyeing the troop as they started walking through the field.

It was true. They could all pass for human. Boss was still the tallest of them, about six feet tall. His hair was black, his skin was tan, but his eyes were still the lightest shade of blue.

Phlegm had pale white skin, brown hair with streaks of gray, and stood at about a half foot shorter than Boss.

Bunny had changed the least of them. Even the points of her ears were still a little up there. And her eyes, though the pupils were now circles instead of diamonds, still glowed a bright orange past her bronze skin. She wasn't much taller than Nathanial. He wondered if maybe she was a teen in whatever terms sprites considered a teen.

"Let's keep moving," Boss called back to Nathanial's slow pace.

"Wait, but aren't we back in the real world?" Nathanial asked.

"Real world," Bunny quoted in a laugh. "It's all the real world, Nate-o-matic!"

"I mean, you guys can pass for human now, but…" Nathanial gestured at their clothes. "I don't know what time period you think you're in."

The three of them looked like something plucked right off a 1600's cobblestone street, with earth-tone baggy shirts and pants, leather boots and belts, and Phlegm sported a rather floppy brown hat.

"It isn't about what time period we think *we're* in," Boss said rather cryptically and kept moving ahead.

"How did you change your clothes, though? I mean, it's one thing to change your skin like a chameleon but how'd you do the clothes?" Nathanial asked in attempt to rationalize the situation.

"It's called a sprite trick, Natey." Bunny smiled and bounce-stepped as she spoke. "Just messing with those funny receptors you got sending signals to your brain behind those pretty browns of yours. Same kind of thing that can make us invisible to you only this one you haven't learned to see through yet."

Nathanial had to jog to keep up with the troop as they headed down the hill's edge. He couldn't help but to smile at the feeling of grass on his fingertips while curiously pondering the salt taste of the air. When he reached the apex of the next hill, he found below him a town that matched its 1600's cobbled stone streets to the clothes that the sprites wore.

Beyond the expanse of white sand beach below, stretched an old-fashioned port town. Shops built mainly from wood hugged the coast for maybe a half-mile. Four massive sailing ships were at port on the far side of the buildings. Nathanial could just see their rope-strung masts swaying above the rooftops.

Nathanial thought he was in one of his dreams. Quickly he scooted down the sandy hill to catch up with the sprites and bombard them with his excited questions.

"This is amazing! Did we like, travel back in time or something?" he asked out of breath.

Bunny laughed, and said, "No cutie patootie, we didn't travel in time. They're in a time bubble. We use spots like these to travel places you can't go by Niche. Humans of this time period are more in tune with our kind. Makes transactions easier."

"Time bubble," Nathanial repeated. "So we didn't travel in time, but what, they're stuck in time?"

"It's just a bubble where space and time move slower, totally natural, no biggy. Just wait till you hear about the ship we are going on! It sails through the—"

"Bunny," Boss scolded bringing them to a stop, "you can't explain everything to him. There's no way a human can understand how to jump a Niche or how a time bubble works or anything beyond their human shortsightedness. These things were lost to his kind centuries ago. We gave up the ability to include them in our lives the day we signed the Crossing Treaty so just—stop. He doesn't need to know anything."

Boss looked a little sorry about his sudden fury but turned without looking at Nathanial and walked on.

Nathanial didn't know what to think. Where did that anger come from? He had agreed to come on this trip, hadn't he? Boss should be thankful, not yelling at Bunny for trying to explain the craziness around them.

Nathanial realized he had fallen behind again and saw Bunny waiting for him at the town entrance. He quickened his pace to meet her.

"Don't let the man get you down," she said patting him on the head. "He's right in a way.

There's no way I could explain everything to you. That would take a lifetime. And you'd have to be a sprite to utilize the info anyway." She started to look around then said, "Hang here a tat."

It was a funny sight to watch Bunny dart from vendor to vendor. Each time she made a trade with a shopkeeper she would return to Nathanial and place a new piece of clothing over his old. There was a large worn-out leather hat plopped on his head. A puffy white shirt pulled over his torso. A pretty cool leather jacket with removable arm sleeves was slung over his shoulders. A pair of black pants that fluffed a bit at the thighs was awkwardly pulled up over his jeans and tied up with a rope belt, then a pair of brown laced-up boots reaching his mid-calf replaced his sneakers.

Bunny's last trade took longer than the rest. It looked like she really had to bargain for the item, which came from an old woman with crazy gray hair and dead seagulls hanging from her shop roof.

Bunny came back with the object wrapped in a furry rag and held it out in both hands to him. With a pretty smile she said, "Happy birthday."

Nathanial took the furry thing with a blush and said, "Wow, Bunny. Thanks, you didn't have to."

"I know," she bounced in reply.

Nathanial just held the gift, looking at it for a long moment. He had forgotten it was still his birthday with all the new things that were happening, and it wasn't just that, he'd never had anyone that wasn't family give him a gift before. He smiled and unwrapped it.

There lay a black leather sheath below a gold and silver hilt engraved with what looked like a hunting scene, or was it a battle? Some of the men seemed to be wearing armor but whatever they were charging toward was not depicted as they spiraled up the smooth surface with their spears and swords. Nathanial pulled the hilt from the sheath to reveal a beautiful six-inch long silver blade that glinted in the sunlight.

"Whoa," Nathanial said, amazed at the sight, "it's beautiful." He thought on that morning when his mom had for the first time suggested he cut the cake. She had never trusted him with a knife before and he didn't blame her. He had been lucky not to stab himself in the eye when he had coughed. And now, a complete stranger was giving him a knife, but there was not a cake in sight.

Nathanial furrowed his brows and asked, "Do you think I'm going to need this for something?"

"Eh, you're going on a voyage. I'm sure you'll have to cut a rope or something. Every good sailor needs a knife." She winked at him. "And here's a little jingle-jingle in case of an emergency." She took one of many tie-string pouches off her belt and tied it to one of Nathanial's pant loops, then waved him forward. "Come on matey, let's scoot!"

Nathanial had been preoccupied sliding his sheath onto his rope belt while he followed Bunny down the dock, so that when he looked up again his jaw dropped for about the hundredth time that day. This time he caught himself and quickly closed it before a fly got in.

A massive ship was getting ready to sail before him. Three masts stood high with many yards still holding tight to their sails. Wooden ramps slanted down to the dock where sailors carried barrels to and from the ship. The crates, too large to carry, were being lifted onto the bow by a pulley system.

"Okay," Nathanial concluded aloud, "this is officially unbelievable." He slapped his cheek several times and blinked while shaking his head.

Bunny put her arm around him and said, "Just the tip of the rat's tail!"

Nathanial walked up a plank with Bunny right behind him. Boss was already on the deck talking in a strange tongue to a large tattooed man who held the tickets but didn't look happy about it. Nathanial found himself staring at the man's black eyes and the large bone in his nose. He reached the top of the plank and the dark eyes looked directly back into his with a jolt. There was not a hint of a smile in those eyes. Nathanial quickly looked away and moved on, pretending he saw something interesting on the far side of the boat.

Phlegm had already taken a seat on a rice bag and kicked his feet up on the mid-mast. Immediately a sailor came up and pushed Phlegm's feet down yelling something in a different language. Bunny rushed over to ease the situation. Nathanial started to follow when a small hand pulled on his shoulder to stop him.

"Don't," a girl's voice said in his ear, "you don't want to draw attention to yourself."

Nathanial turned curiously toward the accented voice. He looked into another pair of dark eyes, but these exuded a kindness and compassion that the tattooed man's never could. She was about an inch taller than him, maybe thirteen or fourteen years old with brown curly hair and a splash of freckles on her olive skin nose. She wore high boots like his own but with tighter pants and a leather vest over her white puffy shirt.

"Are you a sprite?" she asked quietly.

"No, are you?"

She shook her head. "No, but those you came with are," she added.

"How do you know that?" Nathanial asked,

thinking their disguises had been pretty solid.

"A sprite brought me here as well. He used similar tickets to get us aboard. You are like me. There is something we want that they don't."

"Really?" Nathanial asked dumbfounded to find someone else in his situation. "They do this kind of thing a lot? Take kids' wishes away?"

The girl shrugged. "I don't know how often they do it, but what I do know is when something gets in the way of a sprite's job, he or she knows how to get rid of that blockade. And right now it is you and me they are in the process of ridding."

Nathanial groaned. "You think it's that bad? My sprites have acted like they are trying to help, considering the alternative of this big green dude just taking what he wants anyway. Well, help might be too strong a word but I don't feel like they're trying to get rid of me so much as come to a compromise. You see, since my current wish doesn't work for them and they say I'll be sent to the loony bin if I keep seeing them then really it's for the best if we try this exchange thing. That's where we're going, to Midtown, to get my wish exchanged." He wasn't sure why he felt the need to say all that, but her widening eyes during his talk just made everything blurt out.

"I'm going to Midtown too, but I refuse to exchange. You agreed to that?" asked the girl with shock on her face.

A tall man in a black cloak appeared behind the girl. His eyes were in shadow, but his grim mouth sneered with thick menacing lips. Her entire demeanor changed at his presence. She shrunk down into herself and backed away with the man at her side.

"Wait, what?" Nathanial's stomach dropped as he helplessly watched her being led away. He wanted to talk to her some more. He had been excited to find someone like him who seemed to know what was going on and it appeared as though she was about to give him some advice! He needed to talk to her again!

Nathanial looked back to where Bunny had gone to help Phlegm in hopes to ask her if she knew anything about the strange girl and cloaked man that must be the sprite that brought her onboard. Bunny was continuing to calm Phlegm's situation by mocking his leisurely attitude and making the formerly disgruntled sailor laugh. She gave Nathanial a pat on the back when he joined them but Boss came up to his side and bent to his level before he could address Bunny.

"Hey," Boss said with a sigh, "How ya doing?"

Nathanial was a little put off by the sudden kindness. His last interaction with Boss had been cold in regards to Bunny's attempted explanations to Nathanial. Was this Boss's way of saying sorry for having an uncalled-for hissy fit earlier?

"Fine," Nathanial answered shortly, still waiting for the other shoe to drop.

"Look, I want you to stay close to me on this voyage, or at least one of us three. Maybe Bunny. You like her, right?"

Nathanial squinted at him and gave a nod.

"Don't talk to anyone else and try not to make eye contact. Just lie low," Boss said with a wink and a pat on the back.

Just lie low, Nathanial thought. The girl

had said not to draw any attention to himself. What was with all the gloom and doom on this ship? There was only one type of sailor he could think of that should cause this kind of caution.

"What is this, like some sort of pirate ship or some...thing?" he started when he spotted a man with a peg leg and an eye patch clunk by. "No way," said Nathanial in a whisper, staring the man down. Boss snapped his fingers in front of Nathanial's gaze as if to say, *No staring either.*

It was about a half an hour more of securing the crates before the ship readied to make way, but when it did it was quite the sight to see. Massive fabric sails dropped as a dozen men pulled on ropes. Commands were being called throughout the length of the boat and Nathanial had to push himself into a corner to make sure he didn't get knocked over by the men rushing around him. He'd never realized how extraordinary it was to operate such a large vessel solely by the sweat of men harnessing the wind.

However, it didn't take long for the amazement Nathanial felt to be overrun by something else he hadn't taken into consideration: seasickness. They had only been out to sea for maybe an hour. The coastline hadn't even disappeared and yet Nathanial was stuck in another corner with his face hanging over the edge. He'd managed to hold it all in to this point. He was kind of running on an empty stomach as it was, but he was sure it would only take one more big sway to push that last bit of cereal over the edge.

"You don't look so good," said the accented voice of the dark-eyed girl from behind him.

Nathanial turned to see her looking at him pitifully and a rush of butterflies swarmed away his queasiness. It took him a moment to notice she held something small, milky-brown, and possibly food-like out toward him.

The thought of consuming anything just then filled his mouth with watery bile. "I don't feel so good," Nathanial strained the words out before turning back to his beloved corner.

"This is for you," she shook the object in her hands.

Nathanial looked at it again and asked, "What is it?"

"Ginger Root. It will calm your stomach. A few of the newer sailors use it before they get their sea legs. I've been at sea for about a week. I think I'm finally getting mine so I want you to have this bit I was using. Just chew on the soft yellow middle. It's a little strong but it really works."

Nathanial took the root from her hand and smelled it. It seemed kind of familiar. It made him think of the time his mom attempted to make Thai food for their cuisines around the world week. He nibbled it.

"Thanks, I'll try anything at this point," he said with a nose crinkle.

She laughed, then hesitated. "Sorry if I freaked you out earlier," she said with a crooked smile.

Nathanial nodded, still not really able to articulate properly.

"My name's Aliya. What's yours?"

Nathanial swallowed difficultly and said, "Nathanial, but my online friends call me Nathan or Nate."

Aliya nodded and said, "Oh, choices. I

guess I'll just have to see what comes natural when I call for you."

Nathanial laughed shortly and said, "Just as long as you don't get as clever as Bunny. She can't seem to decide on anyone's name."

"Bunny? That must be the girl sprite who came with you."

"Yeah, she's really nice. She gave me a birthday gift," Nathanial said moving back his long jacket to reveal the knife on his belt.

"Oh, it's your birthday?" Aliya smiled and Nathanial nodded. "Happy Birthday!"

"Thanks," Nathanial smirked.

Aliya kept her eyes quizzically on the knife and said, "I guess that makes sense. You made a wish today. Maybe the gift has something to do with that, or maybe she just likes you. Have you known Bunny long?"

"No," Nathanial said with a shrug, "Just met her today. Just met all of them today. You said you've been on the boat for a week? How long do you think it takes from here to get to Midtown?"

"Oh, I haven't been on *this* boat for a week, just at sea that long. I think my sprite is a Nixie. They live on the water. But he didn't tell me how long this voyage would be. He doesn't tell me much of anything."

"Then how do you know so much about them?" Nathanial asked intrigued.

"Ugh, it's a long story. Basically, my father took in an old wise woman when my mom died, to help raise me and my sister, you know? I was just a babe and my sister is only a couple of years older than me. Anyway, she had me call her Mataunte and she used to tell me the best bedtime stories, all about the sprites. As a child, it was easy to believe the stories, even though my papa disapproved. I think he thought I'd grow out of it. But when it came time for me to question things, the stories Papa told seemed just as unbelievable as the ones from Mataunte. I tried to rationalize so I would test them both, and when I'd ask Papa, 'Why can't we do this on that day?' he would just say, 'Because the book says,' without any real specific reason as to why. Yet when I asked Mataunte, 'Why does my foot tingle so bad when I uncross it?' she would say, 'That's the sprite Yireel, come to make and take the tingles to put bubbles in her soup', or I'd ask, 'Why is Papa's hair falling out?' and she'd answer, 'That's the sprite Redouk, come to take his hair and sew it into a fashionable hat.'"

They both laughed.

"Sounds pretty ridiculous," Nathanial said at the end of his chuckle.

"Yeah, but at least she had answers!" Aliya said, her giggle faltering into a serious thought. "Over the years her sprite stories only became more involved. There were battles and governments and laws. I just didn't think she could keep it all straight if none of it was based in some truth. She was the one that had me start my ten-year wish when I was just three years old. It's the most powerful of all wishes you know. I don't think she expected all of this exchange nonsense to apply. In fact I'd be willing to bet it's a new development. Nothing is supposed to counter such a powerful wish. How did *you* know about the ten-year wish?"

"Um, the ten-year wish?" Nathanial repeated.

Just then Boss stepped between them.

"I need to speak with you, Nathanial," Boss said seriously.

Nathanial looked wide-eyed as he followed Boss. He chanced a glance back at Aliya who stared back worriedly.

"What's up, Boss?" Nathanial asked when they stopped on the other side of the boat.

"What did I tell you?" Boss asked in that annoying adult scolding tone.

"Um, stay close to you guys? Bunny was like ten feet..."

"I said not to talk to anyone," Boss cut in.

"I thought you meant the pirate dudes," Nathanial defended.

"No, I meant everyone, and actually, if you need clarification, especially don't talk to that girl."

"What? Why?"

"Because, Nathanial."

"You can't just say *because*."

Boss sighed and pinched the bridge of his nose shaking his head and finally said, "It's for your own good. We are only on this boat for a short time. You're never going to see her again after today so there's no point in making a friend of her. Okay?"

Now Nathanial shook his head. He didn't want to say okay. It didn't make sense. "She's supposed to be going to the same place we are," he muttered.

"They're not," Boss said flatly.

"Does she know that?" he worriedly questioned.

"It's not our business."

They stood there in tense silence for a moment. Nathanial glanced to where he had left Aliya but she was no longer there.

"Bunny," Boss called across the ship and gestured her over. "Keep an eye on him, please," he said walking off at her arrival.

Nathanial glared at Boss's back as he went.

"Uh-oh," said Bunny, "what's big Hoss-Boss done now?"

"Nothing," Nathanial said pulling his glare away.

"You're looking better," she smoothly changed subjects.

Nathanial looked at the ginger in his hand and said with surprise, "Huh. It really does work." He tried to spot Aliya again but with no luck. There were dozens of broad-shouldered backs blocking his view of most of the ship.

"Hey, have you seen the decks below?"

Bunny asked with a nudge on the shoulder.

Nathanial followed Bunny down a darkening stairway. She led him through a skinny hall with a few doors on their left. Every so often there was a glass lamp burning on the wall. The ceiling was low. Nathanial thought it was a good thing he and Bunny were still less than five feet tall or they would be pretty uncomfortable.

Bunny pushed one of the small doors open, went in and waited for Nathanial to join her before she closed it again. They were in a tiny room with only two bunk beds nailed to the wall beside them.

"Um, this is cool," Nathanial said uncertain as to why Bunny had taken him in this room but under the impression that he should be impressed.

"Yeah, can you believe people sleep in here?" Bunny laughed. "I know a couple of sprites that like making and collecting the mildew in sailors' toenails," she said enthusiastically.

"Ew," Nathanial responded.

"It makes for great anti-itch cream," she said with a vigorous nod. "But they have to be careful not to cause foot rot! Anyway,

I need to show you something with your knife." She held out her hand.

"Oh," Nathanial said surprised and reached down to untie his belt.

He handed her the knife. She unsheathed it.

"Hold out your hand," she said holding the blade high.

Nathanial didn't like the look of this. He glared wide-eyed at the blade in the air and uncertainly back at Bunny. She nodded for him to do as told.

He slowly raised his hand, palm up. Bunny suddenly moved the knife above his hand, blade pointing down and dropped it. He tried to pull away but Bunny had gripped his arm to keep his hand in the path of the falling point.

Nathanial screamed, closed his eyes, and anticipated the stabbing. In that moment he wondered why he had lifted his hand. Why had he followed this girl into a dark secluded place? Why did he trust a stranger? Because she had been nice to him? Aliya was right! He was being *rid* of!

But as the moment passed there was no

pain.

Nathanial slowly opened one eye, then the other. Bunny let go of his arm. The blade was hovering over his palm, hilt aiming toward the ceiling, point almost touching his skin.

"Perfect," Bunny said.

"What?" Nathanial muttered.

"It's a battle blade. It only works if you've got real gumption," she said with a quick hit on the shoulder. "Congratulations!"

"Huh? You mean you were testing if I had… gumption?" he asked with a shrug of uncertainty at the word, "and you weren't really sure if this blade would run through my hand or not?"

Bunny laughed and said, "I've seen enough souls to know yours has that special somethin'-somethin'. Don't worry, Nate-a-rooncy!"

"But why would you want to give me something like this?" Nathanial asked thinking back on Aliya's suggestion that it might have something to do with his wish.

"It was a great deal! The seagull lady had no idea what it could do. I couldn't pass it up. Besides, it's something I know you'll find useful, and useful things make the best birthday gifts!" She lifted her hands up like that settled the matter. "Any-who, say 'Brujula'."

"Bra-chu-la?" Nathanial mimicked closely.

The knife twirled on the spot before it suddenly stopped. Then glided down softly to lie flat in his hand.

"Whoa, what was that about?" Nathanial asked a little freaked.

"See the direction it's pointing," Bunny responded.

"Yeah."

"That's the way you're supposed to go."

Nathanial stared at her waiting for more explanation but she seemed to think that was good enough.

Bunny turned and said, "We better get back up top. A storm's a-brewin'." She opened the door and exited.

Nathanial quickly sheathed his new magic dagger, slipped it on his belt, and chased Bunny down.

By the time he caught up with her, they were on the top deck, and the dark clouds rolling overhead blew all other thoughts away.

GET OFF (OR DON'T EVER)

The pirates were in an uproar as they pulled some sails closed and turned others to guide them through the strengthening winds. It was difficult for Nathanial to hear anything that was being called out around him. The crashing of waves and the winds gusting up against his ears were just too great.

Boss and Phlegm ran up beside Bunny and Nathanial.

"It's okay," Boss called to Bunny. "It's almost time anyway."

Boss knelt down to Nathanial and said in a loud voice, "This is very important, Nathanial. I need you to listen to me, okay?"

Nathanial nodded saying, "Yeah, okay."

"You need to stay close to us now more than ever. When I tell you to, you're going to run. Bunny and Phlegm will go first so you can watch and follow. I'll stay by you to make sure you make it. When it's time, it's time. We have less than a minute opening, do you understand?"

"What? No!" Nathanial said shaking his head.

"We're coming up on the Bermuda Triangle," Bunny yelled to Nathanial over the wind and then turned to Boss handing him a pouch off her belt. "And you are going to need this."

Boss nodded taking the pouch and said, "Right, of course."

"Please, will somebody explain the plan to me again in complete sentences this time?" Nathanial said struggling as the rain began to fall.

"We got to get off this boat before we never do again," Phlegm snorted so softly Nathanial wasn't sure he heard the words right.

"What about Aliya?" Nathanial cried out to Boss.

"Who?" Phlegm asked but Nathanial ignored him.

"We can't just leave her in this storm. Especially not if this ship is headed to the Bermuda Triangle. I've read about multiple mysterious disappearances in that place!"

"Look, Nathanial," Boss said obviously trying to be careful with his words. "I told you they have a different path than us. Aliya has been on her's for a while now. There's no changing it. It's the deal her keeper made with her whether she knows it or not. Now come on, we need to get into position."

The three sprites moved up the bow stairs but Nathanial turned away to search the ship for Aliya.

The clouds had completely covered the sun, which had already been low in the sky. It was dark, and the rain poured fiercely.

"Come on, come on," Nathanial whispered to himself and weaved quickly through the crowd. "This is a boat; how many places could you be? Aliya!"

A huge gust of wind took Nathanial's hat off his head. He watched it land by a set of descending stairs and thought about the lower decks. Maybe Aliya was down there. He was headed toward the staircase when he saw Boss rushing toward him and he knew he was about to be forced to go whether he liked it or not.

Nathanial gave one more frantic glance around the ship and he saw her. She was about twenty yards away. She had spotted Nathanial and was trying to get to him but her keeper had ahold of her arm. Nathanial made eye contact with her. She looked desperate. Just then the boat gave a mighty lurch sending a sailor crashing into the stumbling pair. Aliya's keeper lost his grip on her and fell back. She seized the opportunity and fled away toward Nathanial.

Bunny and Phlegm called to Boss, "It's time!" They ran toward the boat edge and jumped.

Boss watched them disappear then looked back for Nathanial. Nathanial held his hand out to Aliya.

"Come on," he yelled taking her hand and pulled her toward Boss.

Aliya's keeper was in pursuit, but Boss didn't have time to argue the situation. He let the two kids pass him and pushed them up the stairs.

"Jump," Boss called giving them a boost over the bow's edge.

Nathanial knew he had done something crazy wrong. He must have missed his minute window. He had jumped off a ship in a storm and was falling down to a watery grave. Worst of all he had pulled his first ever non-cyber friend down with him, stupidly thinking he was saving her.

Aliya gripped his hand tightly in anticipation of the hard watery impact, but before the end could come, odd glitter cascaded around them. Boss pulled them into a cannonball hug and their descent slowed. Nathanial's ears suddenly screamed and ached. No amount of jaw aerobics could pop them. In clear protest of this pain, his vision winked out and silence consumed him.

When Nathanial opened his eyes, he had to fight the disorientation that persisted in clouding his mind. He expected and wanted to see Jupiter on his ceiling. It was the friend that glowed above him in the night, wishing him out of this world dreams, and the symbol that greeted him in the morning to remind him of all the wonders that exploration had to offer. But Jupiter refused to shine upon the flickering metallic ceiling that now insisted on being above him. He was in a lamp-lit room, lying on a small cot, damp and chilled to the bone. Then Aliya's smile appeared over him and the room warmed. His memory returned with disbelief that it hadn't all been just a dream.

"Hey," she said softly. "Thanks for taking me with you."

Nathanial sat up rubbing his head and said, "Yeah, sure, no problem...where did I take you exactly?"

She laughed. "We caught a passing submarine. I guess your sprites arranged a pickup with some buddies of theirs." She gestured toward the sprites across the room.

Boss, Bunny, and Phlegm were back to their original colors and clothes, sitting on some thimbles around a captain's hat. The buddies that joined them looked a little fishy, literally. Their eyes were large and they blinked sideways with nictitating (semi-transparent) membranes instead of eyelids.

Their skin was sporadically scaly, and they dressed in mainly fishing nets with extra seaweed entwined into their pants.

"We're little again, aren't we?" Nathanial groaned.

"Again? I've never been little. This is weird."

"I guess it's harder to shrink when you're being forced under water at the same time. I didn't black out the first time." Then he looked a little embarrassed and asked, "Did you...blackout?"

Aliya nodded, "Oh yeah. I thought my head was going to explode!"

"How long was I out?"

"You came to just after me, as they were putting you on the cot, but then you just rolled over and fell asleep. You slept through the night. You're lucky, I couldn't sleep a wink!"

Nathanial got to his feet and took a few steps toward the table to see what the sprites were doing. It looked like some sort of game with dice, seashells, and a little crab they'd poke with a stick occasionally. Everyone glanced over at him, then went back to the game. He wondered how mad they were at him for pulling Aliya along.

"Ah ha," gurgled one of the fishy men after rolling the die. "And that's how you cull the clam, boys and girls."

Everyone moaned and pushed their seashells over to the victor.

"Again," complained Phlegm.

"That's what we get for playing a Schooner game with a Schooner sprite," Bunny blurted out.

"Alright," Boss said rising, "we should be docked now anyway, yes?"

The two Schooners got up. The victor said, "Absolutely. It's been a pleasure having you all aboard!"

"I'm sure it has been," grumbled Phlegm.

They all moved toward Nathanial and Aliya. The victor was first in line and said chuckling down at Nathanial, "Aw, if little Braveheart didn't finally wake up," and kept moving past them and out through a hole.

The rest moved on without a word. They were definitely mad at him, except for Bunny. She was last and muttered something like, "gumption" as she passed and handed him his jacket.

Nathanial looked over to Aliya and said, "Guess we should follow."

Aliya nodded and they exited through the hole behind Bunny.

Nathanial and Aliya followed at the back of the pack through a long circular metallic pathway. They could only make out Bunny's outline occasionally when she passed under a vent above them. Nathanial glanced up as they went under one of these vents and saw giant human feet walking past. He then ran into Bunny as she had come to a stop.

Nathanial couldn't see what was going on but he heard a squeaky rusty grinding sound that made him figure the victorious Schooner was opening a hatch. Then the light poured in.

Everyone filed out onto the wooden pier at which a full human-sized submarine was docked, towering above them. They had come out on a lower level of the giant pier, on one of the parallel support beams. Nathanial could see holes drilled through many of the beams that would have otherwise obstructed the path to the shore.

"All right my friends, now it's time for

you to do the thing all us sprites hate to do," victor Schooner said, "time to walk."

Boss took the Schooner's webbed hand, shook it and said, "Thanks for bringing us this far. We'll manage the walk."

The Schooner glanced at Nathanial and Aliya. "Yeah sure, just hurry it up. I'd say you only have another few hours before her keeper gets a track on you."

Boss nodded and said, "Then we better get going."

Nathanial and Aliya looked worriedly at each other but kept quiet on the walk through the pier.

Nathanial could only stand the silence for another ten minutes as they passed through grass the size of trees before he blurted toward Boss, "Okay, I know you're mad at me but come on, I couldn't leave her there."

Boss didn't respond.

"She's going to the same place we are. I don't see what the big deal is," he continued to plead.

Boss shook his head.

Aliya grabbed Nathanial's arm and said, "It's okay, you don't have to…"

"No." Nathanial's anger rose. "This is ridiculous."

"You could have got killed or worse kid," Phlegm spoke up. "In fact, we all might still be getting worse if *he* catches up to us."

"What do you mean?" Nathanial asked.

"Stop," Boss said, doing exactly that. The group came to a halt. "Come here."

Boss grabbed Nathanial's shoulder and dragged him far out of earshot.

In a whisper, Boss continued, "You have no idea what you've done. It's just like everything… The way you spoke back at headquarters, the way you look around and talk to whomever you please and say whatever comes to your mind. You're ignorant. You don't know our ways, and if you're not careful you are going to get us killed."

"Well, why don't you try telling me what's going on without lying, or gambling or whatever? Don't say something you know I think means one thing when it really means another. If I'm ignorant it's only because you want me to be," Nathanial yelled back.

Boss stood up straight. He looked

Nathanial carefully up and down.

"What?" Nathanial asked annoyed.

"Okay," Boss said seriously. "You want me to be straight with you, then here it is. I'll tell you what you've forced upon us. I met Aliya a long time ago aboard that ship."

"What? That doesn't make sense."

"Just listen. Her keeper is the Nixie Cyron. Very tricky sprite. Worse than me. Malicious even. I'm sorry Aliya got stuck with him, but Cyron is in his rights to keep her. She made a wish that interfered with the job of a sprite and Cyron stepped in to make the deal for Aliya's contract. He told Aliya something similar to what I had told you to get her to go with him but she wasn't happy with the idea of an exchange. She only agreed that she would go with Cyron to talk to the sprite that had granted her the wish. The thing is, he never planned on taking her to get that exchange, but instead trapped her on that ship. Every day the Argosy goes into the Bermuda Triangle and every day it enters the back-loop adjoined to that town. It's captured in its time bubble. As a consequence, the ship and its crew haven't aged a day in decades. Any new passenger that boards her had better get off before they hit the triangle or they too will become a part of the cycle. Aliya has been on that boat for five years without knowing it and if it weren't for you, she would never have had a chance of reaching Midtown."

Nathanial was in shock. He didn't know what to say.

Boss brushed his dark blue hair back out of his face and said, "Now we have to deal with Cyron. When he loops back he will know Aliya escaped somehow. He will come looking for us. He's not a sprite I want to be forced into negotiations with."

"What should we tell Aliya?" Nathanial asked softly.

"Nothing. It's best just to take her with us to Midtown and find the sprite that granted her wish. I'm sure she's in the same department as yours. No one goes through this much trouble over any other kind of wish. Aliya's wish sprite is the only one who can help her now."

Nathanial nodded somberly. He wasn't sure if he could keep something like that from her, but he didn't want to argue with Boss just then.

"Okay," Boss said with a hand on Nathanial's shoulder, "let's hurry."

The pace of the group was that of a competitive power walker. Phlegm kept complaining about his bunions until Bunny finally said, "That would explain the smell!"

"Bunions not onions you dust-ridden sprite; my feet are killin' me!" Phlegm whined.

Nathanial had kept pretty quiet since his talk with Boss. He could tell this bothered Aliya, but he didn't know how to handle the situation. He'd never had to keep a secret before and this one was huge. He felt like she deserved to know, but he couldn't tell her with Boss around, and he was terrified how she would take the news of being away from her home for five years. Had her family noticed her absence, or was there a memory draft over her home the way there was over his? He tried to formulate a question to Bunny in hopes of getting answers that might ease the blow when it came time to tell Aliya.

"So Bunny," he started already feeling like

it wasn't the smoothest beginning to an unapproved query.

"Yeah pip, what's up?" she asked slowing down to meet Nathanial at the end of the line.

"Um, about that memory draft over my house, so like my mom is just going to think she had a dream that I was missing, right? She doesn't know I'm gone right now?"

"Right, it's kind of like that annoying buzzy feeling you get when you know you're forgetting something but you don't know what!" Bunny said with a solid nod.

"Right, so, what if I was gone for like a month? That'd be kind of a long time for a buzzy dream feeling to keep her satisfied with my absence, wouldn't it?"

Bunny looked at him with a tilted head, looked up to where Boss was about twenty feet ahead and then looked back down at him.

"Well, you're right," she said in a low tone.

"I'm right?"

"You can't be missing for that long."

Nathanial felt a punch in his stomach. If a month were too long, then five years would definitely be noticed.

"People can have up to seventy-two hours to visit through a Niche and have the memory draft hold up. It's rare for a human to stay any longer than that. If they do then it's usually because of some sort of permanent arrangement for one reason or another. The memory draft goes kaput and any friends or family back home have to come to terms with their absence the old fashioned way."

"So we only have three days to get me home?" Nathanial asked astonished.

"Well, two days now, yeah, but Boss knew we'd be done in plenty-a-time. We should reach Midtown this evening and sort it all out. It's much quicker to get you home through wish-granting sprite's methods than it is for us. After all, your wish sprite did get to your house pretty fast after you blew out those candles!"

Nathanial zoned out to reel over how many tricks Boss had played on him in the first few moments of their meeting. How could he ever trust this sprite leading him to his wish's death? Was Boss really protecting him from the big bad headquarters guy that had ways of getting Nathanial to admit his wish? Surely he wouldn't have tortured a twelve year old and Nathanial could stand up to intimidation, well for these high stakes he was willing to bet he could. Was it truly the best option to ask for an exchange or should he have taken his chances back at headquarters? He didn't want an exchange. It was amazing to be outside, to be finally looking forward to the future. Aliya hadn't agreed to the exchange. She had to know a way to keep her wish and maybe that's why Cyron trapped her. He needed to know what she was going to say to her wish sprite. Thanks to Mataunte, Aliya had the inside info, and actually, if Aliya had never been small before then she couldn't have been in a Niche. No Niche, no memory draft. His brain was starting to mush.

Nathanial jogged up to Aliya, ready to talk out their problems together, but Boss held up his hand saying, "Everybody halt."

"What is it?" Nathanial asked freezing with the others.

Boss put a finger to his mouth in demand for silence. Nathanial's fear spiked at the look of intensity Boss exuded. He sensed the unseen danger around them. The path they had been following was low like a ditch. Anything could be hiding in the tall grass forest above them.

"Everyone get together and get down," Boss whispered.

The group did as commanded. Boss opened his wings and flew up a few feet for a better vantage point.

Suddenly there was a popping sound and a spray of yellow liquid shot toward Boss from behind a large grass blade. Boss did a barrel roll to avoid the projectile and dived down to meet the others.

"You guys need to get out of here," Boss insisted, catching his breath. "I'll keep it distracted. Run, and don't stop running until you're within the town walls."

"What is it?" Nathanial asked horrified.

"It's a Bombardier," Bunny answered. "A kind of beetle that shoots acid."

"And eats sprites," Phlegm pitched in.

"Don't be so discriminatory." Bunny punched Phlegm on the arm. "They eat anything our size."

Nathanial and Aliya exchanged horrified expressions.

There was more popping from their right.

"Go! Now," screamed Boss, and they took off down the path just before the steaming liquid splashed where they had just been.

The Bombardier rumbled down into the ditch behind them and began its pursuit, like a tank with six orange legs, two groping antennae, and a large black body behind a shiny orange head.

Boss took flight and did figure eights around side-mounted eyes.

Phlegm had a hard time keeping up with the others. He was hobbling from his bunions and kept tripping up on rocks. Boss's flying techniques only kept the Bombardier distracted enough for the group to get a few yards away, but when it saw the easy target Phlegm presented it positioned itself for another acid attack curling its backside up between its legs.

Boss saw the beetles intent and yelled, "Phlegm, get your slug-butt moving right now!"

There was a quick succession of pop, pop,

pop, pop, as the boiling, foul smelling, liquid sprayed through the beetle's legs, up into the air, and was on an arched path to land directly on Phlegm's head.

Nathanial stopped at the sound and turned to gaze powerlessly at the sight behind him. There was no chance Phlegm could clear from that much acid in time. Within a blink of an eye, the acid hit and a blue streak passed over Phlegm. Opening his eyes with horror, Nathanial saw Phlegm was gone. He imagined the acid had melted Phlegm in an instant, but then he heard a scream. He followed the cry and saw Phlegm on the ground ahead by a tall grass gate. The blue streak returned and stopped in front of the beetle. It was Boss.

Thankfully Boss returned to face the beetle when he did. With Phlegm gone, the beetle had taken interest in its new closest target, Nathanial. It scuttled a few more steps toward him and readied itself for another attack.

"Get through the gate. I'll be right there," Boss said confidently and punched the beetle between the eyes.

Nathanial put on a full speed sprint to catch up to the others and reached the gate with them. Phlegm was rocking and moaning on the ground.

"I think the stinking thing burned off my bunion," he said holding his foot.

"You should thank Boss that's all that was burned off," Bunny said shaking her head.

Bunny and Nathanial helped Phlegm to his feet and they went inside the gate. Boss flew in quickly after them. The gate was manned by a group of sprites who quickly pulled upon a large spoke wheel, closing the woven grass gate, and keeping the Bombardier from following.

"Man, that was close," Nathanial said watching the gate lock into place behind them. "You okay?" he asked Aliya who nodded while catching her breath. He then took in the quaint town around him and asked hopefully, "So, is this it? Is this Midtown?"

"No," Phlegm answered shuffling beside him. "Just a place to fix our bunions, ring the snake, get a drink, and hitch a ride outta here!"

SIMPLY PETRIFIED

The quintet walked through the small sprite town shadowed within woven blades of grass that formed a towering wall around them. Light only barely sprinkled the ground through a leafy canopy from the outside tree cover.

Nathanial had been eyeing the mushroom homes and shops around them curiously for a while until he couldn't help but to go touch one. Something just looked off about them. When his fingers ran across the rough surface he had to ask, "Why do these mushrooms feel like cement?"

"They're petrified," Boss said glancing over at Nathanial. "We are in a town occupied mostly by Petri sprites."

Nathanial took a closer look at the sprites milling about around him. Unlike the town he had first encountered with many different shapes and color of sprites, all of these seemed to be very similar to one another. They had light gray skin, hair, and eyes and wore differing gray variants of clothes.

"I thought petrifaction was caused by silica replacing whatever organic material is decaying, usually wood, right? I just took a course on this subject," Nathanial said looking to Aliya to see if she was impressed.

"Who do you think puts the *silica* there?" Phlegm rolled his eyes. "Such a fancy word 'silica', it's just Petri spit. And that 'organic material' they are replacing is their food. Ah ha! There it is!" Phlegm hobbled quickly over to a building carved into a stone-a-fied tree trunk muttering something about being able to turn the Nile River yellow.

Aliya laughed. "I actually wouldn't mind using a restroom either."

"We could all use a pick-me-up!" Bunny added making a b-line for the building. "I hear this place has great rock cakes."

Nathanial snickered wondering if she was purposely being ironic. They started toward the entry when Boss put a hand on

Nathanial's shoulder to hold him back.

"Let's keep these round tips covered shall we," he said pulling Nathanial's curly hair down over his ears. "Don't want to attract any unnecessary attention."

With a squirm in his stomach, they continued through the door, going under a sign that read: *The Hollowed Trunk*. Nathanial noticed right away that the dozen or so customers were all staring at them as they stood in the entrance. Phlegm apparently had already made it to a toilet, as he was nowhere to be seen.

Bunny put a hand on Aliya's shoulder and guided her away saying, "Come with me if you want to pee!"

Boss looked down at Nathanial. "How about you, kiddo? Gotta go?"

Nathanial crinkled his nose. "I must be dehydrated; I haven't had to go for a while."

"Let's get you fixed up then." He took Nathanial deeper into the room.

In the center of the dark establishment were about a dozen round wooden tables and chairs. There was a small stage in the back with dusty stools stacked upon it advertising its lack of use for some time. Immediately in front of him, however, was the complete opposite proclamation, a tap-lined bar that stretched the length of the room was where the business boomed. All the patron sprites occupied this location. There were two bartenders serving there, and they looked to be the only ones working the entire place.

Boss took one of two open stools that were squeezed between a couple of middle-aged, googley-eyed Petris. Nathanial uncomfortably took the other. He didn't like being stared at. He wanted to leave, but he was very thirsty.

"We'll be quick," Boss said down to Nathanial's worried look.

One of the bartenders came over. "What can I do you for?" he asked.

"We'll just have two glasses of water please," Boss said rubbing his hands together.

The bartender stared at him.

"And maybe some rock cakes, ah, to-go… and five bottles of nectar," Boss added uncertainly.

The bartender stared at him some more. He took a yellow spray bottle from underneath the counter, cleaned a glass with it, set the bottle on the counter, then finally said to Boss, "Don't I know you?"

Boss's eyes flinched side to side. "Um, maybe. I passed through here a few years back."

"No," the bartender chewed on his tongue, "ain't that."

Boss parted his hands up and shrugged his shoulders. "I don't know then. Sorry."

The bartender kept his eyes on Boss as he filled two nutshells with water. He clunked the cups down in front of them.

Nathanial picked up the one in front of him and stared into the contents. It was clear like water but it had little floaters in it. He smelled it. Seemed fine. He sipped it.

"Hey Jet," the bartender called, and the second bartender came over. "This face look familiar to ya'?"

Jet looked at Boss intently. As Boss took his scrutiny, Nathanial noticed the spray bottle in front of him. Its large blaring front font said *Grit the Gook* and in small print below *Your Multipurpose Gook Getter.* Nathanial spun the bottle around and read, *Active*

Ingredients: 99% Lysozyme, 1% Other. And in smaller print at the bottom, *This lysozyme collection is single sourced, producing a high quality product at a lower cost to you.*

Just then, Phlegm rushed between Boss and Nathanial, took up Boss's water and chugged it down.

"Oh man!" Phlegm said catching his breath after the last gulp. "I'm telling ya, I needed that!"

Bunny and Aliya joined them. The bartender took the spray bottle and put it back under the counter giving Nathanial a quizzical look.

"Better?" Boss asked them trying to ignore his current stare-down.

Bunny nodded. "Oh yeah. Let's get some rock ca—"

But before the word "cakes" came out, Jet had dropped a big bag of them in front of Nathanial.

"You know, Chet," Jet said putting a wooden handled case of five yellow jars down next to the bag of rock cakes, "I think I do recall his face."

Boss dropped a few coins onto the bar and

grabbed the wooden handle on the nectar case. "Well, we better be off. Keep the change." He nodded to the two bartenders, put his arms around the group and started rushing them out. Nathanial quickly scooped the rock cakes into his arms and about knocked over his stool from the unceremoniously forced retreat.

As the group exited the door, Nathanial could just barely hear Jet saying to Chet, "But I don't recall if he was blue back then was 'e?"

Outside the Hollowed Trunk, Phlegm grabbed the nectar case from Boss and started handing out the jars. "Aw, you are a genius. I've always said it. Nectar juice!" Phlegm twisted off the top of the jar and took a gulp. He licked his lips. "If I ever meet a nectar sprite I swear I'm going to marry her."

Nathanial and Aliya looked at each other smiling as they uncapped their jars.

"Cheers," Aliya said holding out her jar.

Nathanial clanked his against hers and said, "Bottoms up!"

They took a big gulp together.

"Wow!" they exclaimed and noticed each other's little yellow mustaches. They both wiped their mouths.

"It's like honey, butter, vanilla and...and," Nathanial struggled for the last ingredient.

"Sassafras!" Aliya filled in the blank.

Nathanial laughed. "What?"

"There's a drink imported into my town made from sassafras. It's kind of like root beer. This has a hint of that in the aftertaste."

Nathanial opened the bundle of rock cakes and everyone took one. He was thankful they were not as hard as their name suggested and washed it down with more nectar.

He and Aliya were about to take another drink when Bunny put a hand over each jar. "You only need a smidge of that stuff every few hours. You can overdose on it ya-know. Don't drink it before bed either or you won't sleep a wink. I don't know why this place sells it in such large quantities!"

"For the Odonata," a tall Petri sprite wearing chaps and a cowboy hat said walking up to the group. His long gray hair cusped the broad shoulders of his thick long brown jacket. "You folks look like yer in need of a ride. I'm just the sprite to see for that." He stuck out his hand to Boss and said with a wink, "You can call me Bluet."

The Odonata he had mentioned ended up being a kind of insect that looked very much like a dragonfly with four separate wings and long, skinny, pointy bodies. The difference from a dragonfly was in their heads, which were like a seahorse's, and tail tips, which had a kind of serrated tooth curving down at the end. They were oddly beautiful.

With the size Nathanial currently found himself, these insects were over four times his length. Six of them perched lightly upon and tied to a horizontal wooden beam across from a pond. One of them had dark maroon wings with clear tips. Its body matched its wing color. A second had a shiny blue body with a light hint of blue in its mostly clear wings. A third had a turquoise green body and velvety black wings. A fourth was red with points of black in clear wings. And the last two were yellow with clear wings.

"Whoa," Nathanial said walking up to the maroon Odonata, "we get to ride these?"

He held a hand out to an Odonata and let

it sniff him. He looked closer at the reins latched around the creature's mouth, which strung back to a two-seater saddle on its back. He saw that only the two bigger Odonata, the maroon one and the black winged one, had this two-seater saddle.

"How much for the two big ones and the small red one?" Boss asked Bluet.

"Well now, for just those three it's going to be fifteen gold pieces," Bluet started.

"Fifteen, that's outrageous," Boss protested.

"Now, I ain't finished. You're going to need a handler with ya."

"Oh, of course."

"How else you expect me to get my babies back home? This ain't a human rent-o-car you know. You can't just drop them off at your next stop."

Boss nodded in frustration. "And how much more is that going to be?"

"You'll need to add another Odonata for the handler..."

At this point, Aliya dragged Nathanial off to the far end of the Odonata fence. She seemed motivated to get away from the rising tensions.

"How are you holding up?" she asked Nathanial in a small voice.

"I'm okay," he said really unsure of how he was holding up. "How are you?"

She nodded. "Fine."

The turquoise Odonata beside them sniffed Aliya's hair. She giggled.

"Beautiful, aren't they?" she said petting its nose.

"Yeah." Nathanial nodded.

Aliya glanced over to the loud negotiating voices that were taking no notice of her. "Do you think you know where we are?" Aliya asked in a whisper.

"What?" Nathanial asked surprised.

"I mean," her voice was almost inaudible, "could you find your way home from here?"

Could he find his way home from here? He had flown through a magic hole, jumped off a time-looping ship, traveled underwater to some giant grass shore and was standing in a petrified town where his only clue as to his whereabouts were the sprites around him seemed to have a country accent. And even then, he wasn't sure if that could really tell him anything for certain. They could still be in a foreign country for all he knew.

"Are you thinking of running?" Nathanial gawked.

She smiled coyly. "No." She petted the Odonata affectionately. "Flying."

Nathanial gulped. "I don't know. I've been thinking about it. They know where I live so if I go home their boss will just try and take my wish away by force, you know, by making me tell him my wish. I might be able to handle that, my mom has called me stubborn more than once but it might be better to try and get the exchange with these guys. At least we're guaranteed something that way. What do you think?"

"We can't trust them. No sprite is trustworthy. They do nothing but lie and cheat to get what they want. We have our wishes now. I think we should run if we have the chance."

Nathanial caught Bunny staring at him. He cleared his throat. "We can't talk about this right now."

Aliya took notice of Bunny and straightened up.

"Finally!" Phlegm exasperated. "Let's get

outta here!"

Aliya and Nathanial moved toward the group.

"See if we can ride together," she whispered behind Nathanial's back.

Nathanial's eyes were wide and he swallowed dryly. How was he going to handle this one? He didn't want to disappoint Aliya, but he didn't think they'd last a day away from their sprite troop as tiny easy-to-swallow morsels either. Had Aliya not seen what that Bombardier was capable of? Did she know how to get big again; maybe with Bunny's dust but how would they get a hold of some? He wasn't sure if this plan had been thought through and there was no way to get Aliya alone to continue discussing it before making a rash move.

"Okay," Boss sighed turning to his group. "How are we going to split this up?"

Aliya nudged Nathanial in the back.

"Uh," Nathanial squeaked from peer pressure, "I can take one." He knew it sounded stupid and out of left field but he pushed on. "And Aliya can ride with me."

All the sprites looked at him expressionless.

Aliya nodded with a grin.

Then Phlegm snorted. "Right."

"Yeah," Boss picked back up. "Nathanial, you're with me on the maroon one. Aliya rides with Bunny on the big green one. Phlegm you take the red one and…" Boss turned to Bluet.

"I can pick my own just fine, thanks," Bluet said with a wink. "Let's ride!"

Chapter Six

ODONATA CHASE

Flying on the Odonata felt incredible with the wind in his hair and the scenery zipping by. Nathanial sat in the saddle behind Boss. His seatbelt was a leather strap looped around his back and clasped through a metal ring attached to the saddle.

The four Odonata sped forward just above the grass line. Trees as thick as houses and taller than skyscrapers flew by their path. They swerved around towering flower patches and through holes in fallen tree trunks.

They'd been riding for a couple of hours, and Nathanial still saw things that caught his interest. Little homes spiraled up the giant oaks. Youthful looking sprites chased each other on the backs of hummingbirds or katydids. Even once he spotted a sprite dressed like a warrior standing on a fox's back as it jumped through the tall grass.

Nathanial felt pretty good about his journey. If the worst-case scenario left him back in his room at the end of this, at least he had had these few days to experience something most people wouldn't even believe possible. And he was sure Aliya would be able to sort her situation out with her wish sprite. Maybe she could wish for her family to forget she had been missing or wish she could be put back as if she'd never been missing at all. Would that even be possible?

He thought about it for a while. Aliya would be about eighteen or nineteen years old if she could be put back properly. Would she still want to chat with him online if he asked her? He needed to get her last name if he was going to look her up on Facebook. But wait a second. He really should be thinking about a way to wish for himself not to be stuck in his room for the rest of his life! He couldn't give up so easily.

Nathanial's anger at his moment of complacency bubbled to a boil. He had become more used to his cage than he'd realized. How dare he be thinking of what he was going to do if he returned to that life. There was no going back now. The window of possibilities was open and the view was grander than he'd ever imagined. Knowing he could be a part of it was something that couldn't be taken away. He wouldn't *let* it be taken away!

Just then, something swooshed by his ear. Nathanial saw Bluet, who was in the lead, slump over and dive down into the grass.

"Whoa!" Boss cried pulling to the right with the reins. "What was that?"

Another swoosh flew by Boss's head, but he pulled quickly to the left and something *thonked* into the passing tree.

Boss looked back behind them. Nathanial did the same. Someone was tailing them on another Odonata, one of the yellow ones from the stable. It was someone in a black cloak and they were gaining fast.

"I think our time is up," Phlegm cried out to Boss.

The three remaining Odonata clumped together.

"Give your beasts some nectar!" Bunny yelled to the other two.

"Oh right, like that's easy to do!" Phlegm complained.

Boss reached for a jar out of the saddlebag. "Take the reins," he called back holding out the leather straps to Nathanial.

"What?"

"Hey, you wanted to drive, didn't you? Now's your chance."

Nathanial took the reins as Boss started to scoot up the long neck of the Odonata. Nathanial looked back and saw the cloaked figure pull back on a bow.

"Hold on!" Nathanial cried and yanked the reins to the right.

The Odonata quickly jerked the commanded direction and rammed Bunny and Aliya, who screamed in surprise.

"Sorry!" Nathanial winced.

Boss had fallen flat to grip the neck of the Odonata. "Keep her straight for a moment please," he yelled back.

Nathanial tried his best not to pull on the reins as he looked back again just in time to see the release of the bowstring. He couldn't tell which way the arrow went but it was Phlegm that reacted. With a scream, he disappeared into a thick bush.

Boss had made it to the head of the Odonata. He unscrewed the nectar jar. Nathanial looked to his right to see Bunny's Odonata already sucking up the nectar while Aliya held tightly to the reins.

Then it happened all at once as Boss got the jar to its destination. Their Odonata sucked up the entire contents of the jar, its eyes widened, its pupils dilated, the wings' vibration intensified, its body shuttered, and they took off in a blur.

It was everything Nathanial could do to hold on and nothing Boss could do. He flew back and barely managed to grab onto the toothy tail of the Odonata.

"Ouch," Boss said shaking his cut left hand but held firm with his right elbow now hooked on the tail.

"Boss!" Nathanial cried.

Boss saw their pursuer directly behind them, no longer gaining but still matching their speed.

"Nathanial!" Boss screamed. "Nathanial,

pull up!"

"What?" he bellowed with all his might over the wind.

"PULL UP!" Boss pointed with a bloody hand.

Nathanial pulled quickly back on the reins. The Odonata lifted higher. Nathanial glanced back to Boss for further direction and was petrified with the sight that took him. Boss let go of the Odonata tail.

"Boss!" he cried in shock.

Amazingly, Boss spread his wings and landed perfectly on the head of the yellow Odonata behind them. The cloaked figure was taken aback. Boss only had a moment to turn and grab the outstretched bow before the next arrow was released.

"Nathanial." It was Bunny. She was beside him again at the reins of her Odonata. "Take Aliya."

"Huh?" he was really losing his senses now.

"Take Aliya. Our Odonata hurt its wing. I'm going to fall back and help Boss. You two get out of here." She nodded at him.

Not really comprehending anything he was doing anymore, Nathanial moved without thought or feeling. He reached out his hand to Aliya who stretched out for him. It was tricky as the wings of the Odonata kept them from getting too close. Aliya jumped. Nathanial caught her arm and pulled. She landed behind him and Bunny fell back.

They rushed on through thickening branches and darkening woods. Nathanial let his Odonata do the flying; he just held on in disbelief.

Nathanial felt Aliya's frightened grip around his waist loosen slightly as finally they came out of the woods. A lake spread ahead of them with the colors of the sunset reflecting beautifully in it. The Odonata was exhausted and glided down by the lake's edge to drink.

Aliya slid off the trembling maroon back. She took a few steps toward the water's edge and sat down. Nathanial joined her. They looked at each other and then to the rippling water ahead.

"Now what?" Nathanial finally asked.

Aliya shook her head. "I don't know."

He felt a little annoyed by this answer for some reason. Hadn't she been planning to escape? Shouldn't she know what to do now? "But this is what you wanted, wasn't it?"

Aliya looked hurt at the shortness in his tone. He couldn't look back at her.

"No," she said softly. "Not like this."

"I don't see why not. You wanted away from the sprites, and now we're away from them. What's next?"

Aliya kept quiet for a moment. Then she fired up. "I don't see why you were so keen to stay with them! You can't trust them. Remember that they were taking you to steal your wish away. I'm surprised at you. I would have thought… whatever it is you wanted, what you wished for every day for ten years, and from the look of you that's most your life… after all that, you are so easily giving it away. It must not have been very important."

"It was too important," Nathanial defended.

"Really?"

"Yes, really."

"Couldn't have been."

"It was so."

"Not if you'd give it up without a fight."

"I did fight. I am fighting. I told you. They

said it's the exchange or nothing."

"Well, they lied. And if you knew anything about them you'd know you have to outsmart them to get what you want." She crossed her arms.

"And if you really knew them as well as you think you do then they wouldn't have outsmarted *you* on that boat, now would they?" He regretted it as soon as he said it.

She turned to him quickly. "What do you mean?"

Nathanial bit his lip. "Nothing."

She uncrossed her arms. "Nathanial... Nathan. What do you mean?"

Oh, she was using the friendship card on him with that "Nathan". He felt horrible. What a way to break it to her.

Nathanial sighed and mustered as much sorry in his eyes as he could.

"That Cylon dude," he began.

"Cyron," she corrected.

"Yeah, him...he played a trick on you."

"What kind of trick?" she said with ever-mounting fear in her eyes.

"That boat we were on, the Argosy, it's in a time loop."

Aliya stared at him. He knew she didn't understand.

"*You* were in a time loop," he tried again.

"What do you mean?" she asked but comprehension was lighting in her eyes.

"Until I pulled you off that ship...you were entering the Bermuda Triangle every day and restarting that day without ever knowing you had set sail yet."

"How long?" she said suddenly.

"What?" he said startled.

She stood up. "How long!?"

"Five years," Nathanial said quickly.

She began pacing and pulling her hands wildly through her hair. "It's too late," she was muttering. "I can't stop it now."

Nathanial got up. "Whoa, whoa, calm down."

"What am I going to do? It's too late."

Nathanial stepped in front of her. "It's not too late. Whatever it is, it's not too late."

She froze and tears swelled in her eyes. "You don't understand. My wish. It couldn't have been granted. Not if it's been five years."

"Aliya. We can still fix this. Let's go to Midtown. We'll find the wish sprites. They owe you an exchange at the very least! That's what Boss said, we're owed. You can ask to be sent back home as if you never left, I'm sure of it."

"Ha!" her laugh hit Nathanial in the creepiest pit of his stomach. "That's all I would need. To go back to that life unchanged. My older sister sent to her fate and I to follow. Both to die the same way as our Mother." Aliya wrapped her arms across her chest and began swaying.

"What? Whoa!" Nathanial tried again to calm her. "Look. You obviously need this wish granted. It's probably best if you don't explain anymore. From what I gather that would break your wish and probably the ability to exchange it, BUT, I still think the best way to fix this is to go to Midtown. I don't think running is an option anymore."

Aliya thought on it, nodded her head and let loose of her rocking body. "Okay," she said gathering her composure.

"We better go in case your Cylon got away from Boss and Bunny." Nathanial said approaching the Odonata.

"What?"

Nathanial glanced back at her confused expression. "Oh, I mean Cyron."

"That wasn't Cyron."

Nathanial paused. "It wasn't? Then who was it?"

"I don't know, it wasn't him though, Cyron wouldn't use a bow. He is more fond of knives, nets, and tritons."

"Oh great." Nathanial frowned. "So we have multiple bad guys after us. What do you think bow-guy wants?"

"Nothing good." Aliya looked worried. "He came really close to your head a couple of times. I think you were his target."

Nathanial caught his open mouth, clamped it shut and swallowed hard. "Yeah, like I said, we better get going, *now*."

He started to mount the Odonata but hesitated. "I don't know which way to go," he said with harsh realization.

"Really?" Aliya said walking up to him. "But Bunny told me you'd know."

"Bunny," Nathanial said and put his hand on his hip. "Oh." He pulled out the knife. "You might not want to watch this."

"Why?" Aliya didn't like the look of the

knife.

"Because I don't." Nathanial gulped with uncertainty. He hadn't tried this by himself yet. What if it didn't work?

He lifted the knife into the air and put his palm in its path.

"What are you doing?" Aliya took a step closer.

"It's okay," he said as much to himself as to her. "Stay back." He dropped the blade.

Aliya gasped and threw her hands over her eyes.

"I'm fine," Nathanial assured her, catching the beat of his own heart.

She peeked. The Blade hovered barely an inch from his palm.

"Wow," Aliya said stepping even closer. "How does it do that?"

Nathanial thought about saying his massive bravery held up the blade but instead he just shrugged saying, "I don't know. But Bunny said it shows me the way I'm *supposed* to go."

"Uh, it's pointing down."

"No, I have to give it some kind of command first." He cleared his throat.

"Brogula." Nothing happened. "Bra-jewla." He tried again to no avail. He didn't feel very confident with the way Aliya skeptically looked at him but he tried again. "Brujula!" The blade twisted on the spot, then slowly glided down to lay flat in his palm.

"Neat." Aliya nodded.

"Yeah, except it's pointing south toward those mountains when we've been heading west toward the sunset ever since the attack."

Aliya saw that he was right and bit her lip. "Guess we won't make it there before dark then."

"No. But I don't want to stay out in the open like this, either." Nathanial sighed. "Let's ride a ways south. At least until the sun is under the horizon."

Aliya nodded and they mounted the Odonata.

The last hump of bright orange dipped beneath the western hills. Deep purples were giving way to the darkest of blue and stars were peeking out above.

Nathanial felt Aliya shivering through the

saddle. He knew they needed to stop soon. It was only going to get colder. He spotted orange light speckling up a tree a few yards ahead. Nathanial pulled slowly back on the reins and landed at the base of the large pine.

"There has to be such a thing as hotels in sprite land, right?" Nathanial said jumping off the Odonata. "You can stay here if you want. I'm just going to knock and ask if there's one around." He took off his jacket and handed it to her.

Aliya put it on and nodded appreciatively.

Nathanial went up to the only door at ground level. There was fiddle music coming from inside and the sound of many laughing voices. That had to be a good sign, right? He was about to knock when he noticed a flier by the door.

It read, *Wanted*, in big bold letters. Under it was a bust sketch of both Nathanial and Aliya looking particularly seedy in their pirate disguises. In slightly smaller writing underneath it read, *Reward 1000 gold pieces.* And under that, *Contact your nearest retrieval squad on sight. Detain them yourself if necessary.*

The door swung open. Nathanial froze wide-eyed and guilty at the wobbling old man squinting back at him. His wiry straw beard twitched.

"Who's dare?" he asked through a rank burp.

Nathanial's eyes dodged from the flier to the man.

"Is that you, Batilda? Come to take me up again?"

Nathanial put on his best girly voice and hummed, "Mmhmm."

"Well, I can fly meself, I tells yuh. I do it (burp) every night!"

The old plump sprite pushed Nathanial to the side and started flying in zigzags up toward the treetop then away from the tree and towards it again.

Nathanial quickly grabbed the flyer and stuffed it in his pocket. Before he could remove his hand from his pants someone else was at the door. It was a youthful barmaiden with fair skin, long red hair, a blue plaid dress, white apron, small pointy ears and fierce green eyes.

"May I help you, young Sir?" she asked

wiping a cup with a rag.

"Um." Something was stopping Nathanial's thought process here. "Ah."

"Are you lost?"

"Lost..." He tried to think. Was he lost?

"Do you need some food or a place to rest your head the night?" she tried with a large sparkling smile.

Place to sleep. Yeah, that one seemed right. He nodded.

"Come on in then, dear. We'll get you set up."

Nathanial started to walk in when he remembered. He waved a quick hand for Aliya to come join them, and he entered the tree.

RED HEADS AND BOARD BEDS

The tavern was cozy, lively, and very Irish, if only in the look of it. Most of the couple of dozen sprites scattered among tables and stools were ginger-headed, pale-faced and freckled. They were the most normal lot Nathanial had seen, except for the ears and wings. But even the wings camouflaged well with their plaid clothes.

The barmaid showed Nathanial to a nice half-moon corner-cut table with a colorful lamp burning over its center. He was so enamored by the woman as she wiped the table with her rag that he almost didn't realize Aliya was standing in the doorway looking for him. He quickly signaled her with a somewhat embarrassed wave.

"Oh, will there be another joining you then?" the barmaid asked seeing Aliya uncomfortably making her way through the crowd.

"Um, yeah, sorry if I should have mentioned...is that okay?"

"Of course dear. The more the merrier!"

Wide-eyed, Aliya scooted into the table. She took off Nathanial's jacket in the new warmth of the room and set it beside her.

"Well, you can call me Breann. What can I get for ya then?" Breann said smiling down at them.

"What would you recommend, Breann?" Nathanial asked sweetly.

Aliya looked horrified over at Nathanial, but he didn't notice.

"Tonight's stew is wonderfully hearty and a cup of Jasp is always best before tucking in for the night," she said with a sure nod.

"Sounds perfect," Nathanial said and watched Breann as she walked away toward the far bar.

Aliya hit him on the arm. "Are you crazy?"

"What?" Nathanial said with a side glance to her.

"Do you have any *sprite* money? They just don't give things away for free here you know.

She's not filling us up with *hearty stew* out of the kindness of her *heart*."

Nathanial finally looked over to Aliya now that Breann had exited through a door behind the bar. "Don't worry, Aliya. Of course I have money. I wouldn't have brought us in here if I didn't."

"I'm not so sure," Aliya said pulling her gaze from the same door Nathanial had been staring at. "Where did you get sprite money?"

"Bunny gave it to me."

"Why would she do that?"

"I don't know. In case of an emergency, she said."

Aliya rolled her eyes and crossed her arms.

"Why are you so upset?" he asked dumbfounded.

"Nothing."

"Don't do that. What is it?"

Aliya sighed. "It's only...I get a Nixie from hell kidnapping me onto a boat for five years and you get the Easter Bunny showering you with gifts."

Nathanial couldn't help his laugh but quickly stifled it at her expression.

"I'm serious," she muttered. "Not fair."

Nathanial cleared his throat. "Well, you're right. It's not fair, but you're not the only one getting the short end of the stick. Remember Bow-man wanted my head, and..." He put his hand in his pocket but then thought better of it. Breann was on her way toward them. "Eh, I shouldn't show you now but believe me, even if we aren't on the Argosy anymore, you and I are still in the same boat."

Aliya squinted down at his pocket.

"Here you are babes, hot from the pot!" Breann set down two large iron bowls with mitts that she slid off under them. "I'll be right back with your Jasp!"

Nathanial and Aliya looked into their respective bubbling bowls.

"Looks like meat and potatoes mostly," Nathanial said optimistically.

"What kind of meat do you think?"

Nathanial smelled it. "Not sure but I can't imagine this group wrestling down a cow."

Aliya giggled and reached for two wooden spoons from a utensil cup on the table. She handed one to Nathanial and said, "Well, here goes nothing."

She pressed the spoon into the dark liquid and let it fill to the brim. Nathanial watched her intently as she blew the steam away, pressed the wood to her lips and sipped.

"So?" Nathanial inquired hopefully.

Aliya nodded with surprise. "Not bad."

Relieved, Nathanial boldly tried for a bigger bite of stew. A nice square cut meaty piece. It took the cool-down blowing treatment just as Aliya's had and was shoved into his mouth. He chewed for a while. Aliya watched.

"So," she giggled, "how's the meat?

"Chewy," he stated obviously.

"I think I'll try the potato then." She smiled going in for another dip with her spoon.

Breann returned with two pint-sized foamy drinks in beautifully carved mugs. She slid one in front of each of them.

"Bon-appetit!" Breann said with a twirl back around. She swished her way over to the fiddle-man who'd been on a break, whispered something in his pointy ear and clapped as he started up a tune.

Nathanial was watching Breann take up her dress skirts and fling them about as she kicked to the left or right. Most of the crowd clapped along as they watched but Aliya's only interest was in the new drink before her. "You don't think it's alcoholic, do you?"

Nathanial didn't respond. His chewing had slowed and he seemed to have forgotten how to blink.

"It sounds like an alcoholic drink… Jasp." She smelled it and foam went up her nose. She shook it off.

A dashing redheaded manly sprite took up dancing beside Breann. They clapped and kicked simultaneously. Nathanial now forgot how to chew.

Aliya sipped the drink. "Mmm." She took a bigger gulp.

A good half the crowd were getting to their feet and dancing now. Nathanial's shoulders moved a little left and right with the beat of the music.

Aliya dipped her spoon into the stew and brought up a peculiar looking piece. She narrowed her eyes at it and then widened them. "Um, when she said hearty you don't think she meant *heart*-y?"

Nathanial was humming and suddenly

slid out of the booth.

Aliya was so surprised she dropped her spoon on the table. The organ looking meat rolled off a ways. She couldn't believe her eyes. Nathanial was dancing by the table. She looked around. Everyone was dancing except a couple of girls sitting alone at different tables. She hadn't realized how few girls there were until then. She looked back at Nathanial and was horrified when Breann came over, took up his arm and pulled him to the center of the manly group.

"Well, she really works hard for her tips, doesn't she?" Aliya grumbled to herself.

Aliya couldn't see how this was possible. Sure there could be a popular dance among a small group of people that everyone could get down to together, but no way did Nathanial belong in this group. Yet there he was kicking and clapping at all the right times, swirling about with Breann.

Aliya took another few gulps of her drink but didn't put it down at that. She only stopped to take a breath then downed it, gulping until her mug was empty. She couldn't take her eyes off the spectacle before her. Should she try to save him? Did he need or want to be saved? She glanced over to Nathanial's untouched drink.

Nathanial was having the time of his life. He didn't know how he knew the dance but he was doing it. It had to be Breann, he was sure. She was just such a good dance partner. She must have been leading him and he was just following. He'd read about it but never knew he could do it and do it so well at that! She was beautiful, smiling and twirling and smiling some more.

Her eyes were so green and sparkly. He stared into those eyes as she faced him for another arm hook spin. The world blurred behind her, then for a moment something flickered in her cavernous eyes. Not in the green iris but deep within the black, something like fire. And Nathanial faltered. He missed the next dance step.

"Are you all right?" Breann asked still smiling and hopping on the spot. She tried to take his arm again.

Nathanial looked past her and over to Aliya. Something seemed wrong with her.

"Sorry," Nathanial said pulling away. "I

better get back to my friend."

"Oh, don't worry about her," Breann encouraged. "The Jasp is just doing what it does."

Nathanial pulled his arm away. "What's that suppose to mean?"

"Well," Breann fluttered, "it's a sleep aid, of course."

Nathanial looked back over to Aliya who kept dropping her face toward the stew and jerking it back up again.

Breann watched Aliya amusedly. "She wasn't suppose to drink it all at once and oh my," she giggled unsympathetically, "did she drink yours as well?"

"I'm sorry." Nathanial continued to pull away. "You said there was a place we could sleep tonight?"

Breann looked completely put out. She signaled to a man at the bar as Nathanial ran over to Aliya. He got there just in time to keep her from smashing face first into the stew, but to accomplish it, he had to push the bowl back; it caught on the mitt under it and toppled. Amidst the rolling hearty bits, plain as day, he saw a piece of rat tail.

"Ugh," Nathanial said holding Aliya to keep her from falling into the mess. "Guess that answers that."

An elderly frail sprite with a cane hobbled over. His light orange eyebrows just about covered his eyes. He held up a bronze key with a big wooden plaque hanging off it and the number three carved into it.

"Follow me," he mumbled.

Nathanial picked up Aliya, who thankfully was awakened somewhat by the disturbance and was able to stand. He grabbed his jacket from the bench and threw it over his shoulder.

"What's-goin-on?" she said trying to lift her head.

"It's okay. We're going to bed," Nathanial said putting her arm over his shoulders.

They followed the man through the still dancing crowd. Nathanial glanced back at Breann who'd taken back up dancing with the handsome sprite from earlier. Nathanial thought he suited her better anyway.

They went up a narrow spiral staircase that was carved into the back of the tree. The old man lit the dark path with a candle he held shakily before him. They passed two doors before they reached one that the old man unlocked and pushed open. He handed Nathanial the key.

"Breakfast at sunrise," he croaked and hobbled back down the stairs.

The room was tiny, completely carved into the tree, and only lit by the full moon's light shining through a circular window. A bunk bed protruded from one wall, and on the opposite wall was a little curtain that said *Toilet.*

Nathanial sat Aliya down on the bottom bunk. She immediately slumped over. He helped her legs onto the bed and she rolled over groaning.

Doing a bravery check, Nathanial pulled back the toilet curtain. No serial killer in there, just a closed hole in the floor and a foot pedal.

"Hmm," Nathanial considered it. "Nah, I don't think so."

Nathanial went over to the circular window and gazed out. He'd always liked looking out his bedroom window. He mused that perhaps he'd been a cat in a past life.

Observing the branches below and the low moon in the sky gave him a sense of peace. With a thrill, he lifted the wooden peg from the window latch and pushed open the pane. A toddler taking his first lick of ice cream couldn't have been happier. The cool breeze blew in and Nathanial inhaled the sweet clean air. How many times had he sat at his bedroom window and wanted nothing more than to do that very act? To breathe air that hadn't been circulated through a dozen filters before reaching him. His heart fluttered to imagine himself opening that window with his mother at his side when he got home. She was the only other person in the world that would take as much joy in such a small thing.

He had inherited his dreams of travel and adventure from her and she had given that all up to watch over him. Maybe now they could finally be adventurous together.

Nathanial sighed and took the flier from his pocket. He stared down at it. There was still a ways to go and much to figure out before he could start planning trips with his mother.

Aliya groaned again. He wanted to talk to her about the flier and what she might know about *retrieval squads*. He was lucky to have her, a girl with insight on this strange, hostile world. She was his ally, the only one that shared his plight. Considering her breakdown at the lake he wondered what circumstance could possibly have had a three year old girl wishing for something that was a matter of life and death. If he was having trouble replacing his wish it made perfect sense that she wouldn't even consider the option. No wonder she had wanted to run. If only that was an option, but with that paper in his hand it was more clear than ever that it wasn't.

Nathanial set the paper on the bedside shelf and sat next to Aliya.

"You feel okay?" He whispered.

Aliya was mumbling. Nathanial bent over her turned-away face. She was saying something in another language, but he didn't know which one it was. He could only say it wasn't Spanish because he'd taken two courses in that. He was never exposed to foreigners till this happened, and she spoke

English so well he sometimes didn't even catch her accent. It was strange to hear her like that.

He patted her back and scanned the room. He spotted some quilted covers on a shelf under the window. Nathanial shook one out over Aliya and took the second one up to the top bunk via some foot notches in the wall.

The bed was as hard as a board. No, it was a board. No attempt to soften the carved-out beds had been made. He rolled up his jacket and placed it as a pillow, then threw the thin blanket out over his body and lay down. This was as close to camping as he'd ever come. He smiled and closed his eyes.

THE HOT ESCAPE

Nathanial woke to Aliya shaking him. He could barely see her panicked face. The sun was just on its way up to the horizon and everything was before-morning blue.

He sat up and wiped the sleep from his eyes. "What is it?"

Wide-eyed, she held up the flyer.

"Yeah, that's what I wanted to show you last night. It was by the tavern door," he said putting on his jacket.

"It was by the door!" she whispered loudly. "Nathanial, are you crazy! Why would you come in here if this was by the door?"

"I don't know. I figured we hadn't been away from the others long; maybe the flyer was just put up and no one had seen it yet."

"What if Cyron had them made and it was up all day?"

Nathanial paused before answering. "Well, I think they would have taken it down after they saw it so we wouldn't see it."

"They don't take down wanted posters, Nathanial; they want everyone to see them."

Eww, she had called him Nathanial that time.

"Wul," he mumbled climbing down from the bunk, "I'm sorry, I... I don't know what I was thinking." He faced her annoyed expression.

"I know what you were thinking. Or rather how you weren't thinking, I should say. You took one look into those green eyes and went all goo goo." She held a moment to see the effect of her words and when she saw they hit true she continued. "But I don't think you could help it. No guy could. I'm pretty sure I know what kind of sprites these are and we really need to get out of here before they wake up."

"Why? What are they?" Nathanial switched from shame to fear.

"I'll tell you when we're far away from here."

Nathanial looked out the window at the orange line on the horizon. "They serve breakfast at sunrise. They might be awake already."

"We'll just have to go down as quietly as possible and see if we can get out without anyone noticing." Aliya put the flyer in her pocket, grabbed the key off the side door shelf, and slowly opened the door.

They tiptoed, barely breathing, down the narrow spiral staircase. When they reached the swinging door at its bottom Aliya peeked over into the dining area.

"Looks clear. Let's go," she whispered.

Nathanial pulled her back for a moment. "Shouldn't I give them some money… in case they don't know we are wanted? We don't want them calling anyone on us."

Aliya bit her lip. "Okay. You can leave some coin with the key on the counter, but be quick."

They pushed the wooden swinging-door until it made a squeak, then eased out sideways through the small opening. They weaved soft and swift between stools and tables toward the door.

Aliya set the key down on a counter by the exit. Nathanial fiddled with the strings of the pouch Bunny had given him, trying to get it off of his belt loop.

"Come on!" she beckoned him but the strings were well knotted and Nathanial couldn't get it undone. "Just forget it then, let's go."

"Well, good morning!" A loud and cheery voice came from the kitchen door behind the bar. "Ready for breakfast already! Didn't take you two for early risers."

They stared shocked and guilty over to Breann as she brought out a plate full of glazed biscuits.

"Oh, no, thank you." Aliya was trying to put on her best smile. "I think we have to be going. We would just like to pay for the dinner and boarding."

"Ah, but you can't leave without breakfast. It's included, don't-cha-know." Breann put down the tray on a table in front of them.

Nathanial looked to them hungrily. "Maybe we can take some to go," he said. "How much do I owe you?" He was still fiddling with the knotted strings.

"Let me help you with that, dear," Breann said with that beautiful smile that made Nathanial go blank. He dropped his hands and watched her untangle the pouch from his belt loop. "If you like I'll just pull out what ya owe."

Breann opened the pouch and looked inside. Her eyes flickered back up to Nathanial and he saw the same fire he'd glimpsed the night before. It shook him back to his senses with a spike of fear.

"What-a-ya playin at here?" Breann said throwing the pouch back to Nathanial.

"I don't know what you mean," Nathanial said peering down into the pouch. He reached in and pulled out silvery metallic discs the size of mini Oreos. "What are these?"

"Ya trying to tell me you don't know?" Breann said as her skin began to redden and that flicker in her eyes became a flame.

Aliya backed up and reached for Nathanial when the exit door behind her swung open. The handsome sprite that had danced so well with Breann the night before stood there with three uniformed sprites behind him.

"Perfect timing," he said and made a grab for Aliya but she was a step ahead.

Nathanial was right there with her as it was definitely time to run. They both dodged to the left, around the tables and toward the only door they could think might give them an exit route, the kitchen.

They dove in, Nathanial first and Aliya bumping in behind him. They hit a shelf and sent a dozen pots and pans clanging to the ground. They made a hard right turn only to realize a moment too late they should have made a left.

"The door is the other way!" Aliya yelled catching a glimpse of trash cans standing in front of their exit a few yards to their left.

There was a sound of a table falling in the dining room followed by the kitchen door banging open hard and wide.

Nathanial and Aliya had made it halfway down the kitchen, in the wrong direction, when Nathanial turned to see Breann standing in the doorway. The sight was horrifying. Where there had been long auburn hair now there spiraled fire in deep reds and orange, like the fury in her flaming eyes. Her skin was red and her wings were flared open. She leaned forward and flew at them!

The sight struck Nathanial with such sudden fear, he tripped over his own feet and fell behind Aliya. The silver pieces that had still been in his hand flew in front of him, passed

Aliya, and hit the wall at the end of their path.

Aliya helped Nathanial to his feet. She looked to where the silver bits had hit and saw openings forming where each one touched.

"Let me see your pouch!" Aliya screamed.

"What?" Nathanial asked frantically, still staring at the fire coming at them.

Aliya forced her hand in the pouch and threw a handful of silver at the wall. An exit sizzled open in front of them. They dashed through.

Nathanial and Aliya darted straight for the Odonata. Neither dared turn to see how close their pursuers were. They climbed the saddle ladder faster than seemed humanly possible and before they could take another breath Nathanial slapped the reins that sent them flying into the air.

For a few relieving seconds there was wind on their face and grass passing them by. Then an unsettling heat rushed up on their backs. The hot breeze blew dirt and debris past them. Nathanial glanced back and saw the grass was on fire. Then the trees and the air burst into flame. A rumbling, all engulfing ball of fire was headed toward them.

"Holy crap!" Nathanial screamed.

Aliya searched hysterically in the saddlebag. "Is there any more nectar?"

"Yeah! Yeah, there should be. We had two jars in there!"

She pulled out the jar and handed it to Nathanial. "I'll hold the reins. Think you can make it to the mouth?"

Nathanial gazed up the long neck in horrid recollection of what had happened to Boss when he'd tried that stunt. He didn't think he'd have any better luck than Boss had, but unfortunately, the rampaging fire didn't give him much of a choice.

"Yeah, just keep ahold of this for me, would you?" He unhooked the seat belt from the saddle, clipped one side onto his belt loop, and handed the other side to Aliya.

Aliya put the looped leather of the belt on her wrist and nodded to Nathanial. "I have you."

The heat intensified. Nathanial had wondered once what the sun would feel like on his skin if the ozone layer collapsed and now he felt he had his answer. Still, he held fast to the cool jar of hope and crawled quickly up the Odonata's neck. This put the beast off balance and it struggled to keep its height. It dipped up and down through the grass and narrowly missed smashing into a boulder.

Nathanial reached the panting head. The Odonata shook and the jar slipped in his hand. He caught it, along with his heart that had leaped from his chest. He carefully twisted off the top, keeping one elbow hooked in the bridle and firmly grasped the jar in his free arm. He reached out with the jar, straining to put it by the Odonata's elongated mouth. Why did the mouth have to be so long? It was longer than his arm!

"Come on," he groaned trying to get his arm longer by shifting his body into a crooked angle that put his weight precariously on edge. "Come on!"

Nathanial was sweating, scarily not from nerves or the hard workout. He could smell everything on fire around him. The jar began to slip in his wet palm. His vision was reddening.

Finally, the Odonata got a whiff of the nectar and curved its long anteater-like tongue backwards and into the jar. With a single suck, the nectar was gone, and the Odonata jerked forward with nitro speed.

Nathanial and Aliya screamed. As Nathanial had feared the kick-start knocked him back. He tumbled and bounced down the length of the Odonata, past Aliya, and just before he hit the toothy backside, the belt caught him by the waist and swung him off to the side. The speed of the Odonata kept him bouncing there, attached by Aliya's hold on the belt.

Aliya was in pain. Her body was twisted around and bent down with her arm out toward Nathanial. The belt-loop on her wrist strained against her skin with each bounce. She tried to pull him up but the speed and the weight were too great.

"Nathan!" she screamed. "Nathan I... I can't pull you up!"

Nathanial tried to get his bearings. He kept twisting, and he felt nauseous. He could tell the fire was getting farther away, but his new predicament allowed him no relief. He stuck out his leg on the next bounce and was able to catch his foot on the under-curved tooth. He used his other leg to press up against the

Odonata and steady himself. If he could just get back on top instead of hugging the side he could scooch back up to the saddle.

Nathanial thought back on a rock-climbing book he had read from the "Sports to Try" section of his bookshelf. There was something in there called friction climbing that is used when there aren't good holds available to the climber. It relies on balance and footwork, shifting weight over the feet for grip.

Nathanial licked his lips and felt the weight of the foot that gripped upon the Odonata tail tooth. He knew if he could switch from his right foot to his left then that would open up his options for a better hold with both feet, seeing as his left foot currently swung in the wind giving no assist at all. He held his breath and quickly hopped off his right foot to replace it with his left, then swung his right leg over top of the tail. Hugging, pressing and shifting his weight with his arms and thighs he was able to fully come around to the top of the tail. He pushed his weight off the tail tooth from the tip of his left toe and pulled himself forward. Finally, he was in a position where he could get on his hands and knees to crawl the rest of the way to the saddle.

Aliya looked immensely relieved as she handed the reins back to Nathanial. She took the belt loop off her reddened wrist and stretched her arm out while Nathanial buckled back in.

"Thanks," Nathanial said once able to breathe again. "You saved me back there."

"You saved us first. The fire was right on our tail!"

Nathanial smiled and gulped at the thought. "I need to check the battle blade for directions."

"Maybe in a little while." Aliya looked behind them. "I'm not sure how long that fire ball will keep spreading. Last night the blade had us going south toward the mountain. If we can fly up it a ways, to a viewpoint maybe, where we can make sure the fire isn't behind us anymore..."

"That sounds like a plan to me."

The sun had climbed half way to high noon before the Odonata reached an open rocky viewpoint on the mountainside. It landed on a jutting rock and the two jumped down to stretch and find their course.

"Look at that." Aliya pointed out.

In the distance, they could see smoke billowing from a spot in the pine forest.

"Man," Nathanial gasped, "did we do that?"

"Don't blame us," Aliya said glancing at him. "Those sprites are notorious for starting wildfires. They are also responsible for countless ruined relationships. Mataunte would always say, 'Make sure the boy is seeing the girl in your heart and not the fire sprite on your shoulder. A love started with sudden fiery passion is sure to burn out quick and painful'."

"Wow," Nathanial shook his head. "Sprites ruin relationships and start forest fires too? What don't they mess with, and why do you suppose they even bother with us?"

Aliya sighed turning to Nathanial, looking as if she felt there were a few things he needed to know now. "A long time ago, before recorded history even, the sprites were symbiotic with us. The relationship was beneficial to both sprites and humans. Then, of course, there were a few humans who thought themselves clever and found a way to take advantage of their sprites' abilities. In retaliation, those sprites began to manipulate their humans so it was more beneficial to themselves. Eventually there was a great falling out and the sprites hid themselves from the humans, but they still needed what we had and continued to use us without giving back the way they used to."

"So they became more like parasites," Nathanial said.

"Exactly. But there are still rules they have to follow and that will be our saving grace. Mataunte says if a human becomes aware of the sprite working on them, it becomes almost impossible for the sprite not to give something back. Cyron had found a way around that by keeping me on the Argosy, but your sprites seemed to be upholding the law by taking you for an exchange."

"Their boss didn't want them to take me. He wanted me to give up my wish and go home with nothing."

Aliya narrowed her eyes. "Sounds like their boss is a part of the faction looking to abolish the last remaining human rights in their laws. They've been a kind of secret society ever since the Crossing Treaty war took them and their monarchy out of power. Mataunte told me that when they were at their height, plagues, economic depressions, and civil unrest broke out in human society from their continuous pillaging of us. The sprites with a conscience tried to stand up for us and the monarchy had them imprisoned, or worse, for their protest. When the rest of the sprites saw their own kind being prosecuted over their right to speak freely, they stood up against the monarchy until it finally fell. Some laws were restored to protect a human from overuse but the right to openly negotiate with a human was still deemed unsafe. It's only allowed now if humans accidentally find out about the sprite working on them, hence our opportunity. Thanks to the longevity of sprites though, many of the supporters of the monarchy still live and are trying to restore sprite superiority over humans. They see us as dumb animals and the very thought of negotiating with us disgusts them."

Nathanial gawked. "How does Mataunte know so much about the sprites?"

"Oh believe me, I've asked her a hundred times. She can't tell me. I'm sure she's been through something like we're going through now and if she tells me, something bad would happen."

They both watched the smoke for another moment.

"Well, we better go. I only have today before my mom notices I'm missing," Nathanial said pulling out his battle blade.

"Ugh, I hate this part." Aliya turned her head and closed her eyes.

Nathanial lifted the blade and dropped it toward his hand. It hovered. "Brujula!" he commanded, watched it spin and come down to rest in his palm.

Aliya looked to see where they were headed next. "Looks like we go around the mountain," she said following the point toward the west.

They hadn't been flying long over the boulders and sparse tree terrain when Nathanial brought the Odonata to a sudden halt.

"What is it?" Aliya asked stretching her head around to look in the direction Nathanial now stared.

"I think I see something," he said unbuckling his seat belt.

They jumped down. Nathanial positioned himself behind a large rock and signaled for

Aliya to come beside him. He peered around it, struggling to see past the line of trees.

"Yeah," he said pulling his head back, "there's a road over there and something of a traffic jam. Lots of different kinds of sprites hanging out."

Aliya poked her head around the rock to see. There *were* a line of sprites and what a strange traffic jam they made. There was the animal variety of transports. Foxes, squirrels, rats, raccoons, and a dog made for the furry rides. Owls, chickens, guinea fowls, and a duck made for the feathery transports. Aliya was surprised to also see a few motorized vehicles in the mix, most being motorcycle-style hybrids with wing adaptations for the option to drive or fly. Then there were the riders themselves. Their variety of skin pigmentations could color the rainbow and their clothing styles would make a rather impressive window display for the passing centuries of fashion.

Aliya moved back behind Nathanial. "We must be close to Midtown then."

Nathanial nodded. "I say we keep hidden behind these rocks and follow the traffic up."

He looked over to the large Odonata and sighed. "And unfortunately I think we should let our buddy here go. He's too easy to spot and his wings make too much noise. Who knows how many of those sprites have seen our wanted posters."

Aliya patted the Odonata on the nose with a sad nod. "Thanks for getting us this far pretty boy. You're free now." She removed the saddle and gave him a tight squeeze around the neck. "Go on now," she nudged him away and smiled admiringly at the Odonata's beauty as it disappeared into the brush.

They kept low, sprinting from rock to rock, staying behind trees and bushes until they came to a mountainous rock face that seemed to mark a dead end. The long boulder beside them broke their eye contact with the traffic jam.

"Maybe we should sneak back through that crack in the rock and try to spot the sprites again," Nathanial whispered pointing to the opening.

It was a tight squeeze but they started to make their way through. They came to a point where the crack was thicker above them than ahead, and they had to climb up to get through. It was at this viewpoint that Nathanial spotted the traffic again and the reason for the backup was explained.

"Oh no," he whispered at the sight.

Uniformed sprites stood guard at a large stone arched gateway. The gate had strange block letters carved into its apex and what appeared to be a translation elegantly etched bellow it read, *Midtown*. The guards were checking papers from each incoming sprite, then, in turn, showing them a flyer and asking questions.

A large spotted owl moved on through the gate and Nathanial's stomach dropped at the revealed sight of a broad-shouldered, thick-lipped, troll of a sprite, with colors of the open sea, and dark splotches running up his sharp cheekbones to the points of his ears. Though it was the first time seeing his more ominously-colored sprite form, Nathanial recognized the sneer.

Aliya's eyes widened as they fell upon the same unfortunate sight.

"Cyron," she whispered.

Nathanial's eyes searched the surrounding

gate for an alternate entrance and began to get a grasp of how large Midtown really was. He didn't notice it at first, because it blended so perfectly with the mountain face, but the city stretched up in a vertical slant like it was a part of the mountain. It was beautiful. Buildings were carved into the natural jutting off of the rocks with an artistic flare. Columns and arches, statues and sculptures, fountains and pools, staircases and winding roadways were all form-fitting to the rock.

"This place is massive," Nathanial said gawking eyes moving up to the sky. "It will be tricky, but I think our only option is to climb up the mountain there," he pointed to a spot a football field above them, "where the wall is thinnest. We can use the silver pieces to make an opening. There seems to be, like, a groove there so I don't think we'll be seen."

"But once we get in there how are we supposed to find the right sprites? You're right, look at this place. It could take forever to find our wish sprites and with all those guards in there we are bound to get caught."

"But you said there are rules. Even if we do get caught shouldn't we be able to make a case for ourselves?"

"I'd rather make our case to the sprites who granted our wishes than to those uniforms. Remember there are sprites sympathetic to humans and sprites that see us only as creatures put on this earth to provide them with what they need, and *they* think we shouldn't have any rights at all, just like the old monarchy I told you about. I'm pretty sure a sprite that grants us a wish is sympathetic to us, and a sprite that considers us wanted, like those uniforms, are not."

Nathanial sighed and looked back at the long line of sprites. "Well, we have to try, don't we?"

Aliya was staring at Cyron. "Yes, we do," she said anger filling her eyes. "Let's go."

MIDTOWN

The climb wasn't completely vertical so at least they didn't fall to their deaths with each minor slip-up. But it was tricky enough to grant a scraped elbow to Nathanial who took a spill on a loose rock and put a rip in Aliya's vest when it got caught on a thorny bush concealed between two boulders she was trying to squeeze through. They were very tired and sweaty with more minor scrapes and bruises by the time they reached the sweet spot in the city's wall. They sat down against their goal unable to find shade from the high fireball in the sky.

"I could really use some water right now," Nathanial said panting.

"I think I saw some fountains inside," Aliya said wiping the sweat from her brow with an arm sleeve.

"Those fancy looking fountains? You can't drink from them, can you? It's probably all chlorinated."

"I'm pretty sure the water is from a natural source in the mountain. Fountains were originally built for drinking and washing. This place has to be a few thousand years old. In Rome, there are still fountains you can drink from where the water flows from 2000-year-old aqueducts."

Nathanial stared at her for a moment.

Aliya noticed and shrugged. "Let's go, I'll show you. I'm sure I'm right."

Nathanial reached in his pouch, pulled out some silver pieces and threw them at the wall. The opening dissolved away almost instantaneously with a quick, quiet, crackling noise. Nathanial thought it sounded like Rice Krispies cereal on steroids. The holes did not create a perfect doorway. They had to bend over sideways and step through one leg at a time.

They came through the other side in a short alleyway and walked to the end of it where they could see a small town square. It wasn't horribly busy but there was at least one uniformed sprite patrolling the area next to a large fountain. He bent over to drink from one of the four spouting jars that poured water gracefully from the arms of a marble female sprite. A large muscular winged male statue stood boldly in the center of the pooling water.

"We can't go out there," Nathanial whispered.

"I know," Aliya remarked looking around. "I wonder if there's some way we could disguise ourselves. They know we look like a couple of pirates. If we can just find robes or something."

Nathanial looked down at his pouch. "Well," he said slowly not really liking his idea very much, "we could go through any wall. Maybe sneak into the back of a shop? But I don't like the thought of stealing."

Aliya looked at the pouch as well. "I know. But if they are trying to steal our wishes, I don't see too much harm in stealing some clothes."

"Ugh, I've been going back and forth on that idea in my head and..."

"What?" Aliya asked not liking the sound

of this.

"Well, I mean, who would have thought we could get a wish granted in the first place? You know? We should be surprised we've even had our first wish granted, not expectant. We don't have their powers. If our wish damaged them and they need us to exchange it for one that will benefit everyone then don't you think we should at least try to come up with a different wish?"

"Nathan." Aliya stopped him. "I think I know what you're getting at and just let me explain before you feel any worse about wanting what's owed to you."

"But that's just it. I feel like I have to be one of the luckiest people alive to have this opportunity. I didn't do anything for this. Nothing is owed to me."

"Yes it is." Aliya put her hand up. "It's a condition to the ten-year wish. It can't be granted to just any human. The human has to have served a purpose for the sprites. A very important purpose."

"What does that mean?"

"If you have been granted a wish it's because you've been giving something to the sprites that they desperately need, not because you're lucky. That's what I was talking about earlier. Sprites have been working on you. In fact, I don't doubt it if they caused whatever it is you made your wish against. That's why the wish hurt them. Why else would they be bringing you here to have it taken back? You had to have stopped their exploitation of you."

Nathanial thought about it then said, "Phlegm *was* calling me a factory. But I thought they were just taking advantage of my situation. I didn't think they caused it. Do you really think they made me..."

She put her hand up again. "Stop talking. We are so close to getting everything set right, you don't want to ruin it by saying something you shouldn't. But yes, whatever you wished away, it was only there to begin with because the sprites put it there. Don't feel guilty. They were using you without your permission and without giving you anything in return. They've been doing it to my people for generations. Most of the sprites in my country are war profiteers. Just imagine all the goods they can collect for their cities from the rubble of ours. When I get to my wish sprite I'm demanding my original wish be upheld for all I and my people have given unwillingly to their kind. They owe me, and don't doubt for a second that they don't owe you too. Now let's get some clothes and get moving."

Peeking around the corner again they spotted a clothing shop just two buildings down and hurried along the back alleys toward it. Nathanial made a small crawl-through entrance into the shop and they found themselves in a clothing rack.

"There are some cloaks just there," Aliya said pointing out of the rack to the adjacent wall.

They kept hunched down while moving through the tight racks of earth-toned clothing. Nathanial peeked over some folded pants to keep a look out for the shopkeeper. She was behind a desk at the front of the narrow hallway shaped shop, folding some fluffy sweaters. There only seemed to be two customers wandering around the claustrophobic space.

"Here," Aliya said throwing a black heavy

cloak over Nathanial before putting a dark brown one around her own shoulders.

"Let's get out of here," Nathanial whispered, throwing the hood over his head and turning around. His stomach was knotting with fear and guilt; and as if fate wanted to teach him a lesson about stealing he bumped into a pair of legs.

"You two look awfully conspicuous," the voice above the legs remarked.

Nathanial's heart jumped into his throat. He knew it, he just knew they'd be caught. He slowly looked up, preparing for the worst but instead, the most welcome of faces smiled down at him.

"Bunny!" he exclaimed jumping up and hugging her. "Aren't you a sight for sore eyes? How'd you find us?"

"Shh, shh," Bunny said looking toward the shopkeeper but kept a smile on her face. "You have my dust on you. I could sniff you out anywhere. I'm glad to see the blade guided you well enough. I knew it would. But you two still have a thing or two to learn about how to blend." She took the cloak off Nathanial. "Let's set you up proper."

Bunny did her strange *zip-a-dee-do-da* sprint around the shop until Nathanial wore an interesting patchwork of patterns for pants, a long-sleeved brown and red button-up shirt with zipper pockets down the arms and chest, a navy blue jacket with coattails and a big brimmed hat with a pocket on the side.

Aliya got decked out in a knee-length maroon dress with similar patchwork style pants but tighter, high brown boots, long-sleeved waist-length black jacket and something resembling a squashed top hat that suited the outfit perfectly.

"There," Bunny said looking at her handy work, "a couple of proper Midtown sprite hoodlums if I ever saw 'em." She pushed Nathanial's hat down a little more and fixed Aliya's hair over her ears. "Just make sure you keep those human cartilages hidden, eh!"

Bunny went over and paid the shopkeeper while Nathanial and Aliya waited by the door. Bunny came to join them, opened the door and said, "Let's go get some grub. Boss will be relieved to see you."

They walked through the cobbled square and ascended a set of stone steps that snaked up the mountainside until they came to a café carved into the rock face. There were a couple of tables outside and a sign above the door with flowers grown over it that read, *Middle of the Road Café.*

The inside was quaint, only eight or so tables with accompanying chairs filled the half moon space. There was a glass bakery display with all sorts of pastries, bagels, and breads inside. On top of it were a variety of coffee pots, an espresso machine and something that must have been a sprite favorite in a large bronze spouted container labeled Morning Grool.

The café server was behind the counter, spraying its surface and wiping it down with a rag. Nathanial felt a tug in his gut as he looked at the bottle in the server's hand. He wanted to get another look at Grit the Gook, having formed suspicions and almost concluded that it was the product he was fighting against. The fact that Grit the Gook was one of the first things he'd ever heard Phlegm say while he was bottling

Nathanial's own byproduct, that it was in such large quantities and "fresh from the source" just through his Niche. He took a few steps closer and noticed there was something a little different about this bottle. It was not so yellow and instead was actually more in favor of the green hue.

"Can I see that for a second?" Nathanial asked and received an amused if not perplexed look from the server that slowly handed him the bottle. The cover read *Grit the Gook Organic* and in small print below: *The human friendly Gook Getter.* Nathanial spun the bottle around and read, *Active Ingredients: 99% Lysozyme, 1% Other.* And in smaller print at the bottom: *All lysozyme collections are from multiple natural occurring sources.*

"Huh," Nathanial pondered. It looked like he wasn't the only source for creating Grit the Gook. Maybe this was a good sign. Maybe he could get out of being a factory after all.

Bunny ruffled his hair as he returned the spray bottle. Just then he spotted Boss at the back corner table sipping from a mug.

The eye contact suggested a look of relief in Boss's eyes. For a moment, Nathanial felt warm thinking it was concern that Boss expressed, but then he remembered what Aliya had said. Any joy in seeing him alive was probably due to Boss's desire to revert Nathanial back to a factory and get back to work.

The trio joined Boss and he signaled to the server who then brought over a full tray of goodies. There were three mugs full of brown liquid, three glasses of water and a plate piled high with cream-coated pastries. Nathanial and Aliya immediately grabbed a pastry each and took a thankful bite out of them.

Though Nathanial was hungry he was also anxious to find out what had happened back on the Odonata. He took a gulp of water and cleared his throat.

"Thanks," Nathanial said first, not wanting to be rude. Boss nodded with a small smile. Nathanial looked around and continued. "Where's Phlegm and Bluet? I saw their Odonata go down."

"We had to bring Phlegm here soon as

we found him," Boss said with a sigh. "He twisted his ankle but he'll be fine. Bluet went home and took twice what he was owed for lost and damaged to his Odonata."

There was a moment of silence as Nathanial took another bite. "Did you find out who the sprite was that was trying to kill me?" Nathanial started again hoping he sounded nonchalant. "Is he still..." The pastry was having a hard time going down his throat. He finished his glass of water.

"He wasn't trying to kill you," Boss said brushing back his hair in frustrated thought. "He was trying to knock us all out with tranq-arrows in order to get at you, but he doesn't want you dead. We lost him in the forest."

"He wants to kidnap me!" Nathanial said wide-eyed and then choked on his latest mouthful. The server came over and refilled Nathanial's glass of water.

Boss nodded. "He's from headquarters. I don't know why they don't trust me to get you a proper exchange. They're doing this kind of thing more and more lately, interfering I mean. They don't want to take the risk that your new wish will be as damaging as the first. I've heard rumors of a new sprite in their employment that can wipe memories. I guess they want you to forget your wish and reset you to normal operating status."

"And that wouldn't be okay with you?" Nathanial asked squinting at him.

Boss looked hurt by the comment and said simply, "No."

"But don't you just want to get back to your job?"

Boss licked his lips. "I've not always been a factory manager. There was a time I tried to get human rights back to the way they used to be. It'd be nice not to feel like a thief again. So, no. If I can get you a fair trade, I will."

"But you tried to get me to tell you my wish at first. That would have left me with nothing, right?"

"Right, and I'm sorry about that. It's been a while since I've spent any real time with a human. I had forgotten how much like us you are. You deserve a wish for all you have given us."

"And what if my new wish doesn't let you continue your work? Do you think headquarters will let that happen?"

"They have to," Aliya spoke up. "That's probably why they are trying so hard to keep kids away from their exchange now. If the exchange is grantable, the law must allow it. In the past, they tried to find a compromise in your new wish that still allowed some kind of gain to their kind, but if they are simply wiping memories and reverting us to factories, it sounds like they are tired of negotiating."

Boss looked at Aliya like he'd never quite seen her before. Nathanial could tell he was wondering how on earth Aliya could know so much about sprite ways, but for some reason he refrained from asking. Instead he just looked back over to Nathanial. "Bunny said you would find your way here with a battle blade."

Nathanial nodded. "Yeah, I did."

"Can I see it?"

Nathanial reached down and unsheathed the blade. He laid it on the table and took up another pastry.

Boss lifted the blade and examined it closely. A strange smile came over him and he looked over to Bunny. "Did you know what you were giving him?"

Bunny smiled back and nodded.

"And you tapped it?" He asked lifting a brow.

"Sure did," she said looking at her fingernails and flicking out some dust.

All out of water again, Nathanial took a sip from the mug of brown liquid to wash down the pastry. He squinted from the heat in his throat; he thought it would be coffee, but the strange liquorice taste made him cough. He cleared his throat from what must have been the Morning Grool and stopped to stare at the unsaid meaningful expressions Bunny and Boss were sharing. "What are you two grinning about?"

Boss shook his head. "You could do so much more than look up directions with this blade."

He put the knife back on the table and Nathanial slid it into its sheath with an eyebrow raised. It was annoying how much Boss enjoyed being cryptic. "Well, I figured something called a battle blade might do more than that," he said, not giving Boss the satisfaction of letting him know it bothered Nathanial that he didn't know anything really.

"And as for you," Boss said turning to Aliya who was very surprised by this sudden interest in her, "we saw Cyron on our way into town."

Aliya looked tense. "I know. We saw him too."

"He says the deal he made with your original sprite keeper doesn't allow an exchange."

"What?" Aliya and Nathanial exclaimed together.

"But that was his whole deal!" Aliya continued. "He told me he was taking me to Midtown for an exchange. I said I'd go talk to the wish sprite but I'd plead to keep my wish!"

"I know," Boss said. "He told you that just to keep you cooperative but supposedly by keeping you on that boat your wish was in some twisted way granted. And if a wish is granted that does not impede the sprites then there is no need for an exchange."

"But that's not true! I mean, my wish wasn't

granted, if I had spent an eternity on that godforsaken boat I guess it would be partly granted in the most horrible way, but I am free now and I will be heard by the sprite that granted me my wish!"

Boss nodded. "That's what I told him. I too believe you should have an audience with your wish sprite, now that you are aware of your situation, but he doesn't want the bother. He longs for a life at sea and you are just the charge he needs to keep him there. Oh and you should know," Boss pointed back to Nathanial, "that sprite from headquarters is a tracker sprite, even more ruthless and cunning than Cyron. He'll do whatever is necessary to get you before the law has its chance to see justice. We need to be quick and sneaky once we walk out those doors. Are you ready for this."

Both Nathanial and Aliya sat gawking at Boss, then they nodded with a gulp.

"Whelp," Bunny said finishing her last bit of Morning Grool and popping up, "if we are all freshened up let's say a quick salutation to the toilets before we go another round out there, eh!"

With bathroom breaks over Boss lead them out of the café. He looked up and down the small pedestrian street, saw the coast was clear and signaled the rest of them to follow as he headed up the narrow path. They continued until they hit a large town square. This one had three fountains and a huge cathedral style building at its end. Actually, it was more like many cathedrals atop one another, and the higher you looked the stranger the style as if new architects had come in over the centuries, adding to and remodeling on top of the old.

"That's it," Bunny said pointing to the oddly beautiful building. "That's where wishes come true."

"Or don't." Boss sighed.

Nathanial eyed all the people in the square and saw a line of uniforms in front of the wish building. "How are we going to get in? We can't very well walk through the front door." He played with the silver pieces in their pouch. He had begun to rely on them and took comfort at the feeling of them on his belt.

"We can't put any more holes in this place though," Bunny said looking down at his hand. "Only for emergencies." She winked at him. "No worries. I know people here."

They walked right through the center of the square. There were sprites playing funny stringed instruments, a puppeteer acting out a scene where a human had a sprite on his shoulder, a lady selling hats made from large flower petals and stands with all sorts of merchandise that said *Midtown.*

Nathanial noticed kids his age and younger contrasted to older family members by their lack of color. Did color come with maturity for the sprites?

It would have been all very exciting and wonderful if Nathanial weren't so fearful of the uniforms just ahead. And his fear was only growing, as Bunny seemed to be leading them right into the lion's mouth.

"Quentin the mitten!" she yelled holding out open arms to one of the uniformed sprites. His brown curly hair was crunched tight under his officer's hat and the orange tone of his skin blared out from the subdued boxy authority of his suit.

Nathanial and Aliya looked wide-eyed at each other then back at Bunny's nerve.

"Dust Bunny!" Quentin smiled and accepted the hug joyfully. "What brings you back into town? Cheese giving you a time again?"

"You know it," Bunny said pulling out of the hug. "What are you doing later?"

Nathanial looked around at the other uniforms that didn't seem to be giving him much notice. They were all smiling at the engagement between Bunny and Quentin. He looked back behind them to the middle of the square. Horrified, he saw Cyron leading his own group of uniforms toward them. Then from a far corner he spotted the cloaked headquarters tracker pushing past a nectar seller.

Nathanial pulled hysterically on Boss's coat sleeve. Boss followed Nathanial's frightened stare before looking quickly back to Bunny.

"Oh look at that; the sun's pushing past the hill," Boss said to Bunny pressingly.

Bunny spotted Cyron, who was throwing

off a bag salesman. She turned back to her buddy trying to keep cheery and said, "Well, Tin Tin, you better be here when I come out if I can't grab you later."

"I will be. Don't forget to check your group in," Quentin called. Bunny pushed on through the doors to the cathedral building with Nathanial and Aliya frantically following on her heels. Boss entered last and locked the doors behind them.

They sprinted down the hall. They passed a registrar's office where a sprite yelled at them to sign in but Bunny called back, "It's okay, it's me! I'll sign us in when I get back,!"

They burst through another set of doors into a large marble room with dozens of half-cylindrical spaces carved in the walls, all labeled with golden letters and glowing with light from an unseen source. Boss paused only a half second to close the doors. Nathanial read the golden blurs in his hurry to keep up with Bunny. "First Star Floor", "Shooting Star Floor", "Wishing Well Floor", "Eyelash Floor", and finally, directly ahead, his heart skipped a beat to see, "Ten Year Wish Floor".

Bunny came to it first, entered the space without a beat and shot straight up into the air. This caused Nathanial and Aliya to stop cold with necks craned toward Bunny's flight up the tower. Their attention was snatched back by a *bang* behind them. They swished around to see Cyron with a group of uniforms burst into the room.

"Go!" Boss yelled and pushed both Nathanial and Aliya into the space.

They couldn't help but hug each other as the intense force pushed them upward. Nathanial felt like he was inside one of those message sending pneumatic air tubes he'd seen in the movies. In this case he and Aliya were the message but there was no tube, just an indention in the wall.

Aliya kept her eyes shut tight but Nathanial squinted up to watch a dozen balconies pass by. The shrinking of the pursuit team below was also shrinking his fear until Cyron pulled a large gun-like weapon from beneath his cloak and pointed it skyward.

Boss rushed at Cyron, about to tackle him before the shot, but a group of uniforms surrounded him and pushed him to his knees. Cyron pulled the trigger sending a massive dark ball projecting out from the weapon. It spun open revealing itself to be a massive net.

Nathanial gawked helplessly up at Bunny's growing figure. Her eyes were panicked and she dropped to the ground, stretching her hand out to Nathanial. He raised his arm in frantic hope and glanced below to see the net was already upon them. It swallowed them in midair, wrapping and constricting their mobility. Their ascent dramatically stopped and they lurched before hurdling back toward the ground.

The net's rope retreated into Cyron's gun and it reeled them in like trapped fish. Aliya, seeing the triumphant sneer upon Cyron's approaching face, began to scream, push, kick and tear at the net confining her. This put Nathanial into a predicament. Should he attempt to aid Aliya in pulling free from the ever-tightening net or stop her from unintentionally punching and scratching him?

They hit the ground at Cyron's feet before Nathanial had time to react and for the first time he understood the phrase *seeing stars*. The net fell loose and Aliya was wrenched away from his side. He stumbled to his feet and shook his vision clear. Cyron was pulling Aliya away toward the exit. She was dazed but shaking it off. She found her footing and screamed at Cyron giving him an almighty kick to his calf.

"Stop!" Nathanial called and chased after Cyron. "Let her go!"

He reached Cyron, grabbed Aliya's arm and quickly found Cyron's hand pushing down upon his face so hard he crumpled to the floor. Realizing harshly he was no match for this beast he looked pleading back to Boss who was still surrounded by uniforms.

"Boss, please, can't you do something?" Nathanial called over to him.

Boss looked sadly to Nathanial with eyes saying he wished he could but obviously he was in no position.

Then Bunny appeared in a shimmer by the exit doors where a few uniforms still guarded the path. She said something to them and they closed the exit doors and put themselves in the path.

"Get out of my way," Cyron said on approach to the guards.

"Sorry Sir, but I can't do that," said one of the guards who Nathanial thankfully realized was Bunny's friend Quentin.

"This human belongs to me. I am in the right. You all have seen the wanted posters," Cyron said pulling Aliya firmly by the neck in front of him to show them her face.

Aliya kicked Cyron in the shin and said, "I don't belong to anyone, you filthy sea serpent!"

Cyron tightened his grip on her and shook her hard while angrily saying, "Let me pass."

"Like I said," Quentin said firmly, "I can't do that, Sir. It seems you haven't formally signed the transfer lease of keepership and this human has a hearing scheduled. You are more than welcome to plead your case at the hearing or, if not, I have orders to escort you off the premises."

Cyron sneered at Quentin. Bunny stepped forward with her hand outstretched. Cyron looked her up and down with an ugly glare then grudgingly threw Aliya at her.

"Fine," Cyron growled. "Have your little

hearing. It's only a waste of time. She *will* be mine at the end."

Bunny took Aliya toward Nathanial who put his arm around her and they walked to where Boss was getting to his feet. The uniforms dispersed and let them enter the airlift.

"This way," Bunny said as they touched down on the appropriate balcony.

Nathanial held Aliya's hand as they walked through a kind of chaos. Their surroundings were like nothing he had ever seen. There were dozens of winged female sprites flying about a white space, all with long flowing hair tied in white-ribboned braids and loose soft clothing that could be a dress or pantsuit or shorts; he couldn't tell with the way the clothes seemed to be shifting constantly. It was like everything else in the room. Constantly shifting. The images that hovered before the sprites were of boys and girls from all walks of life speaking in whispers throughout the space but their lips were not moving.

"Here, you guys get in there while we set things up," Bunny said waving them through a side door that Nathanial could have sworn was not there a second ago.

Nathanial entered the new sparse room and came to a halt as the door closed behind him. Shock was setting in. His struggle with Cyron had left him feeling helpless. He had no control, and after walking through those shifting halls filled with sprites everything seemed so unreal around him. Then he looked to Aliya. She was sitting on the only piece of furniture in the room, a white couch. She was the only real thing he had in that moment and her eyes gazed down, unseeing.

Nathanial sat down beside her. The expression on her face focused the blur in his mind onto her. He'd never seen her lose it like this. The girl who knew everything. The girl he'd come to rely on and believe anything was possible because of.

"You okay?" he asked softly.

She shook her head.

"I think we'll be fine now. We're here. We made it, right?" Nathanial encouraged.

"I don't know. Cyron is here too. You heard him. He says he is in the right. What if he tells them I can't have an exchange? What if they send me back with him?"

"They won't," Nathanial said putting his hand on her shoulder.

"You can't know that," Aliya said looking to him with water in her eyes.

"Look," Nathanial said seriously, "if they do send you back, I will just have to come pull you off again."

Aliya smiled softly. "That's really sweet of you Nathan, but only a sprite can find the Argosy." She looked away, closed her eyes, and a single tear ran down her cheek.

"Well, don't think about that because you made it here to talk to your wish sprite knowing that you can outsmart these sprites. You know so much about them Aliya, I'm sure you can figure this out. Just remember all those things Mataunte taught you. She prepared you for this moment. You have a better chance than me of getting out ahead."

"What do you mean?" Aliya said looking up concerned.

"I have no idea what to ask for in exchange for my old wish," Nathanial said with a small laugh.

"Really?"

"Really."

"Ugh, if only we could tell each other our wishes."

"I know. My circumstances are bad but it's not a matter of life and death like yours is. Don't worry about me. It's not the end of the world if things go back to the way they were. Except now I think I'll feel more like a prisoner than ever."

"Then that is serious," Aliya said wide-eyed. "You have to think of something that will keep them from using you the way they have been. If only we could change their laws."

"What do you mean?"

"Well, right now we are up for an exchange because our wishes have interfered with the jobs of the sprites around us. So they are appealing to the wish sprites to take it back and give a less damaging wish so they may resume taking what they need from us but the contract of the wish is still fulfilled. If we could change the law that gives sprites the right to take from us what they need without our permission or compensation then we might be able to fix many problems at once. Unfortunately it would only apply to humans who have seen the sprites by circumstance like we have, as sprites aren't allowed to reveal themselves in normal situations, but it would be a start. I mean, they already have to agree to an exchange if a human becomes aware of their sprite so this would just be an amendment!"

"So I should wish for sprite law to include that if a human has seen a sprite then the sprite must obtain permission and provide compensation to continue the use of the human?" Nathanial said screwing up his face trying to figure it all out.

"I think so," Aliya said beginning to smile.

"Well, if that works I definitely won't be giving them permission to work on me anymore!"

Aliya laughed. "Me either."

"See, I knew you could figure it out," Nathanial said nudging her. "I will wish for that and then whether or not you're allowed an exchange, my exchange will solve both our problems!"

"Right," Aliya said with relief and hugged him.

At that moment the door opened and three sprites came in. Boss was a relief to see, but the appearance of Cyron and an unknown sprite behind him sent a glob of worry into Nathanial's stomach. Both he and Aliya stood up.

"Hello Nathanial Thatcher and Aliya Levine," said the womanly sprite with a touch tablet in her sparkling sapphire-toned hands. She seemed to be scrolling through information as she swiped the screen downward. "You can call me Jewels. I'll be hearing Aliya's case and ruling on the outcome." She smiled up at Aliya who looked very put off.

"I'm going to go with you Aliya, to speak on your behalf," Boss said stepping forward. "There needs to be a sprite for your case and one against. Cyron is obviously against. Nathanial, Bunny will speak for you and Phlegm must speak against. Don't be too hard on him; he is here representing the best interest of the company after all."

Nathanial nodded but absolutely felt contempt toward Phlegm. Not as much as he was feeling for Cyron however. His gut was writhing with disdain of Cyron and for the hungry glare he was giving Aliya. If only Nathanial could take him down he'd do it in a heartbeat.

"Nathanial, if you'll just have a seat, my colleague Gem will come collect you shortly and take you to your case room. Aliya, if you can follow me please," Jewels said turning toward the door.

Horrified, Aliya looked over to Nathanial. "Don't worry," he whispered in a hug, "We have it figured out. You'll be fine no matter what happens with them."

Aliya nodded and left with Jewels and Cyron. Boss hung back for a moment at the door. He looked at Nathanial and seemed to really want to say something but all he said was, "You'll be fine," and exited, closing the door.

Nathanial didn't feel like sitting. He paced the room and recited out loud what his exchange wish was going to sound like. He wanted to make sure he worded it right. He knew how tricky wishes could be and how words could be twisted. More importantly he wasn't doing this only for himself anymore;

he was doing it for Aliya. He had to get it right.

Then the door opened and a pretty, petite, winged sprite, with golden hair and skin, entered saying in a small voice, "Nathanial Thatcher?"

"Yes," Nathanial responded straightening up.

"I'm Gem. I'll be hearing your wish exchange case and ruling on its outcome, but your wish sprite is detained and thought you might like to observe your friend's hearing while we wait for her. Would you follow me please?"

Nathanial's heart jumped into his throat as he followed the little sprite out the door. He was going to see Aliya's trial! He imagined the look on her face when she was granted her wish and was able to go home. These were the wish sprites after all; they were compassionate toward humans. When they realized Aliya's wish was a matter of life and death they would let her have it on the spot. They wouldn't send her back as a prisoner of Cyron's. Cyron didn't have a chance here.

These positive thoughts only solidified as

Nathanial followed Gem through a golden room with statues of sprites and humans. One statue was of a female winged sprite putting a crown on a youthful man. Another was a female sprite holding up a girl as a golden crutch fell from her side.

"This way," Gem said opening a door and letting Nathanial pass through.

Chapter Ten

CHANGING EXCHANGES

Nathanial found himself at the back of a small crowd. He could see they were standing at the top row of five tiers slanting down into an oval enclosure. He peered around the fluffy feathered outfit of the sprite in front of him and saw Aliya standing next to Boss down below in the oval. Cyron was across from them. If an invisible triangle connected them all, at its third point hovered a glorious sprite with a tower of purple curls upon her head and Jewels stood at her side.

"But why did you not sign the lease of keepership if you knew you were rightfully entitled to Aliya?" Jewels asked Cyron flatly.

Nathanial smiled. It seemed to be going in Aliya's favor thus far.

"There are many parts of the world where verbal contracts between two sprites are still

190

considered binding enough," Cyron sneered. "The girl's keeper knew it was time for her wish to be granted and when that happened she would be taken from his charge. He afforded me the opportunity to ensure her wish fulfilled while keeping the factory in the fold of the sprites."

"Let us clarify these grounds," Jewels said swiping her tablet. "Aliya, if you could state your ten-year wish for us please."

Aliya cleared her throat. Nathanial felt his insides wrench. Was this a trick?

"If it pleases you," Aliya said confidently, "I'd ask that you state the wish and I will confirm or deny. I'd hate to render my wish null by stating it."

Jewels smiled. "Of course, but so you know, you are safe in these halls to speak your wish without revoke. But I will read what is on your file for purpose of ease. It shows a blood curse passed down maternal lines. It claimed your mother. You wished this curse removed."

"Yes," Aliya said lifting her head high. "If what I've been told is true, the blood curse kills its host within a few years of their eighteenth birthday and only after a tortured life of failed endeavors. My mother was murdered in the army when she was twenty thanks to this and as everyone must serve in the Israeli army at age eighteen. My sister is there serving now; if the curse hasn't killed her already. My wish was supposed to stop the curse before it was our time to serve, so I don't see how it could have truly been granted. If your idea of keeping me from my inevitable end was to trap me on a time looping ship then so-be-it, but that does not save my sister and keeps the curse actively demolishing my dreams."

"What Aliya is saying," Boss spoke up for defense, "is that the ten-year wish's obligation to end the curse was never fulfilled. She is still owed that wish for if it were granted then Cyron has no right to her. His imprisonment of her seems more like a continuation of the curse than the release from it."

"Whether the girl likes the arrangement or not," Cyron growled, "her former keeper did abide by our law by giving her to me. The curse can only spread through time and aboard that ship time is not a factor, thus allowing the curse to progress no further."

"According to this, Aliya's former keeper's only job was to aid the blood curse. I'm not sure what benefit he or our kind received from this." Jewel stated questioningly toward Cyron.

"A blood curse is only set upon a treasonous blood line." Cyron snarled. "He was acting out of loyalty to the sprite who was betrayed by this one's kin. As for sprite use, he bottled the worry that the knowledge and expectation of the curse create and I have taken up that role in his stead."

The crowd around Nathanial murmured.

"Punishing the child for the sins of the parent has long been abolished," Jewels said horrified.

"That it not my concern," Cyron rolled his eyes disdainfully. "I am not the one who placed the curse, which is older than that law. I am here to claim my right to the girl so I may return to the sea and continue to bottle her worry. I am being of service, breaking no law, and only wasting my time here. This dry air begins to crack my skin."

"Enough," the purple haired sprite said, speaking for the first time as she glided down to Aliya. She cupped her hands upon Aliya's cheeks. "My dear Aliya. I heard your wish and longed a decade past to find a way of granting it, but alas a blood curse can only be drawn out by the one who put it there. I had not the power to end the curse but I could do something about your suffering. Once you qualified for the ten-year-wish I did as much as I could do toward granting it, for one by removing that awful sprite from your shoulders. He had made you ill when he could. He put holes in your clothes and pulled at your hair. He had whispered horrid things of you in the ears of those that would otherwise have been your friends. I told him he had done enough, his time was up, and I would make sure he'd be lucky to even find work in a dreg cave after what he'd done to you. He told me he had known I would be coming for him and so he'd triggered the final stage of the curse…that you would be dead within the year."

There was a great gasp in the room. Nathanial felt light headed. Gem put her arm under his to stop his swaying.

"He said if I wanted you to live, I would let him give you to Cyron. He wanted you to suffer forever and thought this would accomplish that but I knew you would not. Secretly I thanked him for finding a solution to his own terrible actions. You would not suffer from what you did not know. On the Argosy you would not know you were living every day the same as the day before and I would know you were, at least, living with hope thinking you were on your way to talk with me. That gave me some comfort."

The room was quiet. Water swam in Aliya's eyes. Cyron smiled.

"Now there is a new hope I want to give you, something to ease your worry," she glared at Cyron. "Your sister is not afflicted by the blood curse."

There were more murmurs from the crowd. Aliya's eyes widened. "How…?"

"I cannot be sure why; your records are not complete but I do have my suspicions. It's enough for you to know she is alive and her life is her own. I knew your ten-year-wish extended out to her and so I removed any sprite from her the same day I removed yours. This is all the power I had toward fulfilling your wish and therefore that is what was granted."

The wish sprite backed away and stood tall; clearly mustering her strength for the next words she had to speak. "Aliya, you must return with Cyron. It is the only way to keep you alive."

"No," Aliya cried. "That's not living. That's purgatory!"

Gossiping exclamations rippled through the peanut gallery of the trial. Jewels had to raise her voice to be heard over the shifting bodies.

"Unfortunately, I have to agree with wish sprite Ametrine," Jewels somberly stated, lowering her tablet. "Keepership of the factory known as Aliya Levine is granted to Cyron. The exchange is denied. This hearing is closed."

Cyron strode triumphantly toward Aliya and took her arm in his gauntleted hand.

"Hey," Boss said holding onto Aliya, "You got what you wanted. No need to be rough with her."

Nathanial didn't realize that he'd already run down the tiered room until he was jumping into the space of the hearing. Aliya saw him. Hope cascaded over her face.

"Nathan!" She yelled, "You have to stop this! Make the exchange! Please, you have to stop this!"

Nathanial did want to stop this, but he wanted to stop this now not at his hearing. He painted his target red and charged at Cyron. His fists were balled as Cyron pulled Aliya toward an open door. Nathanial had almost reached Cyron when uniforms blocked him and Aliya was pulled from sight.

"Let go of me!" He screamed but uniformed hands swept him from the room.

"Nathanial," a small voice tried to calm him as he struggled, now being guided down a hall. "Nathanial please calm down. We have to go. It's time for your hearing."

Nathanial pulled free from the uniforms grasp and focused on Gem. Her words were delayed reaching him but when they did, so did his determination.

"Right, let's go," he said resolute to make his exchange and stop this madness.

Nathanial followed Gem while reciting his wish exchange in his mind. It was more important than ever that he got this right. That pompous satisfaction on Cyron's face was burnt into the back of his eyes and he needed to scrape it out.

When they entered the hearing room it was not at all like what he'd just come from. There was no place for a peanut gallery and the circular room had cushions in the center. A massive colorfully glowing glass chandelier hung above. Phlegm was kicked back on a few of the cushions and Bunny was sitting cross-legged and rocking on a big round pillow.

"Feel free to sit where you like," Gem said walking in behind Nathanial and over to a table where she picked up a tablet much like the one Jewels had had.

Nathanial went over and sat by Bunny who nudged him with her shoulder in greeting. "Hey," she whispered in his ear. "Hope you don't mind I requested a private hearing. Thought it might help you concentrate."

Nathanial nodded fervently. "Thank you."

"Of course you sit over there," Phlegm

grunted at the two bonding figures, "I'm the enemy here right?" he asked rolling his eyes.

Nathanial was in no mood to pet Phlegm's hurt ego. Phlegm was in Cyron's position which absolutely made him the enemy, whether he saw himself as the bad guy or not.

"Shush up, ol' Phlegm bucket," Bunny said scrunching her nose at Phlegm, "Natey needs to think what he's going to wish for and guess what, he wouldn't have to if you would have just let him keep his old one."

"Hey, I'm doing him a favor. He can't live the normal life he's been aching for if he's seeing a bunch of critters no one else can see. Trust me Nathan. Exchanging your wish is a good idea. I just hope you know to make it good for everyone concerned this time. I did hurt my leg trying to get you here safe you know. I'd hope that'd earn me a little gratitude."

"Don't listen to him, Nathan Shmathan," Bunny said with a nudge. "You've given his company enough. He's no concern to you, okay?"

From behind Nathanial appeared another

sprite. She passed by them and went to the center of the circle. She was beautiful with creamy skin that sparkled yellow, long dark hair that flowed around her sheer wings, pale flowing clothes that matched her skin tone and shimmering gray eyes. She looked over to Nathanial with a smile.

"Hello, Nathanial Thatcher," she said soothingly. "I'm sorry to see you here so soon after your granted wish. These cases seem to be happening more frequently these days and I can't say I enjoy them." She looked harshly over to Phlegm.

"Hey, stop interfering with our jobs and we'll stop pestering you," Phlegm said lifting his hands as if his point was the simplest thing in the world to manage.

"And what about our jobs, Phlegm?" she said gliding in front of him. "We listen to hundreds of wishes every day, all day, searching for that wish powerful enough to condone granting and after ten years of this boy's life in suffering, suffering because of you, with only one wish he ever made, we finally are able to give what he asked for, having met all the criteria we set forth, and what do you do? Pull him here in front of me to have it ripped away from him."

Phlegm swallowed hard. The sprite backed off and went over to Gem. They looked at the tablet together. Gem stepped forward.

"Because of the decree that any wish interfering with the job of another sprite may be called into repeal, dismissed and re-negotiated, we have called Nathanial Thatcher's presence here to clarify his circumstance and ask him if there is any wish he may now state to circumvent the wish in repeal."

Everyone looked at him but he felt like a computer with a bogged down hard drive.

"I'm sorry?" he said looking over to Bunny.

"What wish do you want for your exchange?" she whispered to him.

"Oh, right." He cleared his throat. This was it. This was the moment to set everything right. This would free Aliya from Cyron, and himself from his room. Together they could find the sprite that put the blood curse on Aliya and have it removed. It could be done. But his mind was wandering and he needed to focus. Nathanial started slowly…

"I wish that the law pertaining to the use of humans as a means to their livelihood must include that if a sprite has been seen by its human then permission must be obtained from said human for the continued use and the...the…" His throat was drying and he didn't like the expressions forming around him, "permission and compensation, yeah, the human must be given something in return for the—use," he really didn't like that Phlegm was now shaking his head, "permission and compensation. That's it. Did that make sense? It's an amendment."

Phlegm sat up and shook his finger at Gem saying, "You know good and well Miss Gem, a human can not make changes to sprite law even with a wish."

Gem nodded, "I know that Mr. Phlegm, unfortunately, Nathanial did not but now I'm sure he is aware, thank you. Nathanial, there are certain rules to the wish exchange. Is there something you want that only pertains to yourself?"

Nathanial was horrified. He didn't know what to do. He hadn't expected this not to work. Rules to the wish exchange, how was that fair? Panic struck him. Aliya would be trapped on the Argosy forever and he would never travel the world, his mother would grow old as a lonely recluse cursed to take care of him forever, and it would be all his fault.

"This isn't fair!" Nathanial protested. "How can you do this to us? You shouldn't be able to just take, or do what ever you want to us without asking. Your laws are bad."

Phlegm rolled his eyes. "Laws are generally made to aid the ones making them and unfortunate for you these laws are for the sprites. Permission and compensation? You're trying to get out of being a factory! It's not possible, kid. It's sprite law and only a sprite can change sprite law."

"Then I wish to be a sprite!" Nathanial said in rebuttal.

Everyone froze, staring at him.

He continued with growing anger. "What? Is that not possible either? What rule is there stopping me from that? If there is one let me hear it!"

Nathanial was tired of being told what he couldn't do. If he needed to be a sprite to change sprite law then so be it. And he could find Aliya this way too. Hadn't she said only a sprite can find the Argosy? He didn't know what it meant for the rest of his life but he knew right now he had no control over anything unless this wish worked.

Gem was whispering in low tones to the wish sprite.

"You can't seriously be considering that wish!" Phlegm protested.

"Why not?" said Bunny getting to her feet by Nathanial. "It has been done before."

"When?" Phlegm said sitting up straight.

"We all can make the choice to be whatever we want to be, isn't that right, sis?" Bunny said looking over to the wish sprite who smiled and glided forward. "No difference if you're a sprite or a human, that is the same. You work for it, you got it!"

"It's true," said the wish sprite smiling fondly at Bunny. "But looking at you now little sister, I say you didn't stray too far from the wish business after all."

"Wait a second," Phlegm said looking back and forth between Bunny and the wish sprite. "Cheesecake and Bunny are sisters?

That ain't fair. I demand a different sprite for the factory!"

The wish sprite looked coldly to Phlegm and said, "Only those dearest to me call me Cheesecake, Phlegm. I'm still Citrine to you. And you're going to have to make a better case as to why Nathanial cannot be a sprite if you want this wish withheld too."

"Well, it's obvious, right? If he's a sprite I can't very well keep him a factory, can I?" Phlegm said obnoxiously.

"But if he's a sprite he will be contributing to our society in another way so he's not depriving us of service anymore by not being a factory," Bunny said with a smile on her face.

"Well, what am I supposed to do for a job then?" Phlegm asked annoyed.

"You and Boss could be his mentors! That way you aren't losing your jobs; you're just adjusting them." Bunny nodded.

"What about all the people at the processing plant!" Phlegm said sure he had her this time.

"They can go into import and use rotating lysozyme resources for Grit the Gook Organic. All the civilized companies are switching! Kids are only meant to get sick on occasion. Stop being so lazy," Bunny said crossing her arms with her point. "And besides, it's becoming quite the trend to be a human friendly producer."

"So it's true," Nathanial said gazing fiercely at Phlegm, "you did cause me to be sick my entire life, just so you could make some stupid cleaning product out of my loogies!"

"Now wait just a second here," Phlegm said in defense. "Just because my gift is for getting some good lysozyme enriched snot outta ya doesn't mean I choose the factory I work in or for how long. That's a headquarters call. And besides, you had that weak immunity thing all on your own; headquarters just maybe exploited it a bit, but it's your own makeup, that's what makes you so irreplaceable!"

"Honestly Phlegm, is that what you tell yourself so you can sleep at night?" Citrine asked seriously. "The boy's immune deficiency was resolving itself once his mother sterilized his room and his doctor specialized his vitamin regimen at age three, but your continued work on him kept this action from being a success. I only needed to pull the trick off his eyes to stop your work and let his natural immunities kick in. Without you and Boss, the boy is cured."

Nathanial stared at Phlegm who was perhaps genuinely shocked and speechless but Nathanial didn't care. How could someone knowingly be harmful to another living being that way? Citrine was right in accusing Phlegm of deluding himself. That would be the only plausible excuse, besides blatant cruelty, for making a living off of someone else's pain.

Gem cleared her throat and Nathanial broke his glare off Phlegm to look at her.

"That would be acceptable," Gem said looking from her tablet. "It fulfills all requisites for a wish exchange."

"But," Phlegm said half-heartedly.

"Are you sure about this?" Citrine asked Nathanial who looked amazed at the verdict. "It's a big change and like Bunny said, you will have to work for it. You would go to school with other sprites and find your way in a very different world and for a time you will be stuck between the two worlds. It's not an easy transformation.”

“But growing up really isn’t easy anyway,” Bunny said with a shrug.

Nathanial swallowed deep. He knew there was no way to fully comprehend what he was getting into with this wish, but for some reason he felt it was the correct course of action. How else would he break out of his room? How else would he find Aliya? He needed to do this.

“I’m sure,” Nathanial said.

“Then that settles it,” Gem nodded. “The exchange is granted. The former factory Nathanial Thatcher, will henceforth be a sprite in training, to be guided by Boss and Phlegm on his journey into our society. Congratulations Mr. Thatcher on your upgrade. This hearing is closed.”

“Oh, headquarters isn’t going to like this,” Phlegm said shaking his head.

A GROGGY HOMECOMING

Nathanial's mind was buzzing. He was being escorted out of the case room and back through the golden hall. Bunny had her arm around Gem telling her what a good job she had done. It seemed Nathanial's case had been her first. Phlegm was still mumbling about the ruin of his livelihood and Citrine was walking very closely behind Nathanial. He could feel her examining eyes on him.

"So what happens now?" Nathanial asked her, keeping his eyes to the floor. "Are you taking me to some place where you change all my molecules from human to sprite?"

Citrine giggled, "No, my dear boy. The differences between you and I are not so great as that. It will take time for you to change. You may have noticed differences in Bunny from myself but if you spend enough time with her you will see even she has not gone through a complete transformation. You must be patient. There is much for you to learn."

Nathanial didn't want to be patient. He just wanted to find Aliya. He couldn't stand the thought of her being on that boat with that evil keeper again. So much of her life had already been wasted there. His thoughts broke. Boss was walking towards them. He jogged up to meet him.

"Boss? What happened? Did you stop Cyron from taking Aliya?" Nathanial blurted out.

"Unfortunately not," Boss spoke sadly putting a hand on Nathanial's shoulder. "It was worse than I feared. Until we know who put the blood curse on Aliya, she is safer where she is." He squinted down at Nathanial and took a step back. "There's something different about you."

Phlegm grunted, "Yeah, you don't want to know."

Boss looked to Bunny who was beaming. "Our li'l NateTastic's going to join the ranks of sprites like us!"

"What?" Boss asked looking to Citrine.

"It's true," Citrine answered. "The exchange has been granted. You and Phlegm have new positions as Nathanial's mentors. He will be a fine sprite one day." She smiled down at Nathanial who was anxious to see Boss's reaction.

"This is unbelievable," Boss said pushing his hand through his hair. "This is legal?" He looked then to Gem.

"Bunny made a very good case for Nathanial. All the criteria are met." Gem nodded.

"Cheater." Phlegm shook his head. "Our sweet Bunny here used to be a wish sprite. No wonder she knew the hoops to jump through. I still think the big man at headquarters is going to have a fit. Not sure he'll let this slide. We had the biggest lysozyme factory on the east coast!"

"Well," Boss said sighing, "we better be on our way back to headquarters to break the news. We need to have Nathanial home today." He looked over to Citrine. "Do you mind if Nathanial uses your transport? It will take too long any other way."

"Wait," Nathanial said looking at them all. "I still get to go home?"

"Of course," Boss said. "You don't become a sprite overnight, I'm sure they've told you." He looked to the rest of them wonderingly.

"Yeah, I guess they said it will take patience and some school but I'm still not really sure what all this means," Nathanial said shrugging.

"That's why you have mentors and Boss will be very good for you," Citrine said putting a light hand on Nathanial's back.

"What am I, chop liva?" Phlegm mumbled.

Citrine pulled Gem aside to speak about the transport and Bunny started teasing Phlegm. Nathanial took the opportunity to whisper privately with Boss.

"Look, a big part of why I did this is because I can't stand the thought of Aliya on that boat again. How far do you think they've got? If you could just take me toward the Argosy now..."

Boss shook his head. "Nathanial, I can't do that."

"Why not?"

"Cyron has it out for all of us now. We put him through a lot of trouble. I'm sure they're halfway to the Argosy already. By the time we catch up they'll be shipping off and if he sees any of us near that boat again he'll have us arrested before we even set foot on the deck."

"I have to try, Boss. If you can't take me now I will find a way myself eventually."

They looked at each other intensely for a moment.

"And when you get her off that boat, then what. What will you do about the blood curse?" Boss asked seriously.

"We will find the one who put it there and

have them remove it. Aliya was practically raised by someone that knows everything there is to know about the sprites. She has to know who did this. Aliya did not do the crime she is being punished for. If we can find the one who placed the curse, surely they will see this is wrong and remove it, but for right now I have to go get her, mainly because of what she said. You heard her, it's like purgatory on that boat! She's going to be living every day not knowing how long she's been there, not knowing if her family is still alive, not knowing if she's been forgotten. I can't stand the thought of it, Boss. I just can't."

Boss held Nathanial's determined expression with contemplative concern.

"All right," Citrine said stepping between Nathanial and Boss, "it's all set for you, Nathanial. Gem will take you home. It was wonderful to meet you and I'm so glad your exchange will be of some good use to you. Not all children are so lucky anymore. I fear that is why my sister left the wish business and why so many are thinking to do the same. I'm just glad she kept an eye on you for me." She bent down and kissed Nathanial on the cheek then headed past him and shimmered away through the golden wall.

Bunny gave Nathanial a big hug. "I'm going to pop in on you in a while to see how you're getting on, okay Nate-a-roony! Don't forget to slide off those sprite clothes before Gem sends you off. Have a good trip home."

She started to walk by but Nathanial grabbed her hand. "Wait, Bunny." He didn't know quite how to express how much he appreciated all she had done for him. Thinking of the battle blade, the silver pieces, how Bunny was always open to answer his questions and most of all how she fought for him in his wish exchange case. Though the words felt small he said, "Thanks. For everything."

She smiled, holding his eyes and taking in all the unsaid things there between them. She nodded and turned away, dropping Nathanial's hand and shimmered into the wall the way her sister had.

"Okay, well, there went the favorite scarecrow that you'll miss most of all and it's time Tinman and I got the heck out of here too," Phlegm said hobbling toward the door.

"Are you going to be okay?" Boss asked Nathanial.

"I have no idea," Nathanial said honestly.

"It might be a couple of days but you'll see me again soon. There's lots we have to sort out back…"

"Back at headquarters," Nathanial finished for him. "Yeah, I know."

"See," Boss said with a small smile, "you're learning already."

He started to turn away but stopped when Nathanial said, "Kind of ironic don't you think?"

"What's that?" Boss asked looking back.

"When this thing started you were so keen on keeping me in the dark about everything. Now you're going to be my mentor."

Boss nodded with a small laugh. "Yeah, it is ironic. Even more than you know."

Nathanial furrowed his brows at the comment. "Why did you have to go and say that? Now you know you have to tell me, right?"

"I would," Boss said thinking on it. "But you'll know why yourself some day…if I mentor you right." Boss winked and his smile spread to the largest grin Nathanial had ever seen on his face. It was handsome but very annoying.

Boss exited out the large door behind Phlegm.

"Let's get you home," Gem said from behind Nathanial.

Nathanial turned and followed Gem through

a small side door. They went down a narrow set of stairs and came out in a shapeless room. It was like the wish room where the walls seemed almost liquid and always changing. Everything was a pale smoky texture. Nathanial held out his hand as some of the ceiling started to drip down in front of him. When it touched his palm it shot back up to its proper place above them.

"See the circle in the center of the room?" Gem asked.

Nathanial hadn't until she mentioned it, but there was a silver circle in the room. Nathanial nodded.

"Go stand in it," Gem said pulling her tablet back up to her face and scrolling through it.

Nathanial did as told and put himself directly in the center of the silver. Getting a sense that this was about to be his path home he said, "hold on a sec. I need to pull off these clothes real quick." Being thankful again to Bunny, this time for keeping his original clothes under all his different disguises along the way, Nathanial eventually stood back up in his jeans and t-shirt. The only thing missing was his sneakers, but he didn't worry too much about his mom noticing their absence. She'd rolled her eyes at them when he opened them a week before his birthday. She had thought them another absent minded gift from an absent father.

"Now, I want you to think back on your first wish," she said still looking at the tablet.

"My first wish? Ever?" Nathanial asked watching the smoky liquid around him.

"Yes. I need to establish a connection. The first wish should pull up the entire file on you."

Nathanial bit his lip trying to remember.

"Close your eyes," Gem said looking up at him.

Nathanial closed his eyes. He could hear a slight humming. It was getting louder. And a little, "cough, cough".

"Shh, shh, it's okay, my baby." It was his mother's voice.

"Mom?" Nathanial said opening his eyes and seeing her face hovering larger than life in the cloudy mist above him.

"Good," said Gem, "we have a connection."

Nathanial watched his mom in the air above him. The image cleared from the smoke and he could see himself as a toddler in her lap. There was a cupcake in front of them with two candles on it.

"It's time to make a wish Nathanial," his

mother was saying.

Little Nathanial coughed again. His mom kissed his forehead and wiped his hair back.

"I know what I would wish for you," she whispered in his ear. "I'd wish you to be well." And she kissed him again.

He could see his little eyes staring into the candle, listening to his mother's words, and he remembered thinking them to himself at her advice.

The images began to change in rapid succession. Every wish Nathanial had made. When he saw a shooting star out the window, when he pulled an eyelash from his cheek, and every single birthday. The room was full of his voice over the years repeating the same thing over and over, "I wish I was well. I wish I was well."

Then the images stopped on his last birthday. Had that really only been a couple of days ago? He was in front of the big number twelve birthday candles with his eyes closed tight. He stared at the look of sorrow on his mother's face as she watched him.

"All right, we have a location set for you, just... wait, you can't be in here!"

Nathanial looked quickly over to Gem's

suddenly panicked voice. It was the tracker from headquarters in a long black hooded cloak walking swiftly in from behind Gem with his dark green complexion, fury in his black cold eyes and a bow in his hand. He wiped his palm over Gem's face. A powder flew over her and she passed out, crumpling to the floor.

Nathanial wanted to run, he tried to run, but the silver under his feet had climbed up his legs and kept him glued to the spot. He started to reach down for the battle blade but with a sickening realization, he glared at it atop the pile of clothes just out of reach.

The clouds were thickening all around him. It was harder and harder to see the approaching sprite. Nathanial pulled at his legs ferociously. The sound of his own voice became deafeningly loud in the room, "I wish I was well." He covered his ears and looked to the tracker sprite one last time, seeing his bow outstretched and the arrow flying through the swirling mist. Then, there was nothing.

"Nathanial." The male voice sounded small and far away. "Nathanial, can you hear me?"

Nathanial opened his eyes. There was an

older man hovering above him. He recognized him. He was a doctor.

"He's waking up," the doctor said.

"Oh thank god." His mother, Suzy, appeared over the doctor's shoulder. "Nathanial I was so worried. How do you feel?"

Nathanial cleared his throat and tried to sit up.

"No, don't get up just yet." The doctor pushed him back down.

It was coming back to him now. Doctor Ferguson. He must have had another bad spell. Doctor Ferguson always came to the house after a bad spell.

"Did I faint again?" Nathanial asked in a cracked unused voice.

"Yes," Doctor Ferguson said getting to his feet, "but I think you're going to be fine. You've been out cold for a few days but you weren't coughing in your sleep like usual. After looking at your promising blood work yesterday we cracked your door open to see if you'd have a reaction. So far not even a sneeze. I'm very optimistic." He smiled and patted Suzy on the back.

Suzy sat down on the bed in place of the doctor. "You were talking a lot though. Do you remember any of your dreams?"

Nathanial furrowed his brows in thought. "Maybe. I don't know."

"Just make sure he gets plenty of liquids and keep him on a diet of bread and crackers for the next twelve hours or so. Let him work back up an appetite on his own," Doctor Ferguson said heading toward the door.

Suzy got to her feet to go shake the doctor's hand. "Thank you so much for coming."

"Oh, not at all..." The doctor's voice faded down the hall as Suzy escorted him out.

Nathanial reached over for the glass of water on his bedside table. He felt an ache in his side and examined the place under his pajama shirt. There was a large bruise there with a thin scabbed cut in its center. Nathanial harrumphed and started to gulp down his water. The sensation made him feel odd. It reminded him of being so terribly thirsty not so long ago but he couldn't grasp the memory. He put the empty glass down and examined himself further. He was pretty banged up.

Suzy came back into the room.

"Mom," Nathanial said looking at a scrape on his elbow, "how'd I get this?"

"Doc says it's a rug burn from when you fell.

We found you in the corner of the room. You took some books and DVD's down with you, so it must have been a bad spell. You have quite a few bruises too." She rubbed his hair back out of his face. "I'm going to get you another glass of water and some toast. You're going to have to stay in bed for a while but doc says I can leave the door open as long as you're not coughing." She smiled giddily at the notion, picked up the empty glass and left the room.

Nathanial sat up with a cracking stretch. Something was bothering him. He had just been told that his door had been open all night, that he hadn't been coughing, that he was doing fine… and yet the corner of his room where the DVD shelf met the bookshelf was of more interest to him than this news. Nathanial found himself staring at that particular corner and went over to investigate.

Suddenly and very unexpectedly an envelope slid out from the very crack he'd been staring at. It fell to the ground and came to rest on his toes. He bent down and picked up the inch-long parcel, took it over to the window, opened the curtains and let the mid-day sunshine in on it. He opened it and read the scribbled words upon the very small piece of paper.

Dear Nate-o-rama,

Sorry about the fuzzy feeling in your head. Looks like the tracker sprite did some damage when we all ditched. The effects of his arrow should be temporary since they didn't get you to their mind-sucker over at headquarters, and we won't let them either! Citrine is having a fit over what happened to you. Even worse we can't seem to find Gem. There's going to be a hearing and we need her testimony. There's some conspiracy theories going around about the old monarchy clawing its way back to power with some sneaky infiltration methods. Gem would be a target for helping you instead of reverting you if that's the case! I don't know. Just take it easy for a while. We'll come and get you for school when this is sorted. I'm sure to pop in on you before then, though.

With Love,

The Dust Bunny

P.S. Boss says he's got your battle blade and he'll show you how to use it properly when we get you.

P.S.S. This letter will automatically destruct in 5,4,3,2

And the paper disintegrated into tiny little dust particles before Nathanial could blink. He stood there for a moment. The words he'd just read felt as dusty as the particles on his fingertips. He shook the thoughts of waking dreams from his head and sat on the thick windowsill to pine out at the beautiful day.

"While I was in the kitchen buttering your toast I had a thought," Suzy said coming in with the toast and a knife on a small plate. She sat down beside him and held up the knife. "I think you should cut the paint."

Nathanial looked at the knife, then to the window.

"It'd be nice to have some fresh air in here don't you think?" Suzy smiled.

Nathanial took up the knife like a prisoner finding the key to his jail cell and sawed the seam of his window frame with gusto. The paint flecks showered down like snow. When a minute had passed he admired his work and beamed at his mom.

"You sure about this?" He asked her.

"The doctor said your white blood cells finally look normal, but if you want to wait another year," she shrugged jokingly.

Nathanial lifted the hooked latch and pushed open his windows. The summer breeze tousled his hair and filled his lungs. He waited for the cough, but none came. Suzy wrapped her arms around her son and they looked out the window together. He could feel it then. This was the first day of the rest of his life and he had some planning to do.

~~THE END~~

P.S.S.S. Not The End